# FIGHTING MAN

**Center Point
Large Print**

**This Large Print Book carries the
Seal of Approval of N.A.V.H.**

# FIGHTING MAN

## ERNEST HAYCOX

CENTER POINT PUBLISHING
THORNDIKE, MAINE

This Center Point Large Print edition
is published in the year 2006 by arrangement with
Golden West Literary Agency.

The text of this Large Print edition is unabridged. In other
aspects, this book may vary from the original edition. Printed in
Thailand. Set in 16-point Times New Roman type.

ISBN 1-58547-745-1

Library of Congress Cataloging-in-Publication Data

Haycox, Ernest, 1899-1950.
   Fighting man / Ernest Haycox.--Center Point large print ed.
      p. cm.
   "Originally published as Fighting man in serial form in West magazine. Originally published
in book form as On the prod."
   ISBN 1-58547-745-1 (lib. bdg. : alk. paper)
      1. Large type books. I. Title.

PS3515.A9327F54 2006
813'.52--dc22

                                                        2005033851

# FIGHTING MAN

## CHAPTER I

In the crisp brightness of a spring morning the Transcontinental, aristocrat of trains, rolled slowly into Crowheart and stopped with a slight sighing of brake shoes. As on all other mornings the mail and express car doors opened to emit mail pouches and odd pieces of freight; and also as usual the half-dozen idling citizens around the spare handtruck—designated as Buzzards' Roost—tried to look wild, woolly and mean for the benefit of the tourists who stared through the car windows to verify their dreams of a West with hair on its chest.

A boy in a sailor suit put his nose to a pane and shrieked, "Mama—cowboys! Lookit'm wearin' guns!" A camera shot through a window suddenly raised and Topeka Totten, most inveterate of Crowheart's loungers, hooked his thumbs into his gunbelt and assumed the popularly conceived attitude of an uncombed outlaw from the hills. Topeka was a harmless, useless soul and this was a game he delighted in. A thousand times he had met the trains, and a thousand times cameras had snapped him. His technique was practice-perfect.

Standing there, skinny shoulders hunched forward as if he were about to shoot the train off the track, and with an ominously evil leer on his alcoholic face, he was the absolute answer to a tourist's prayer, a masterly reproduction of the hard man from the wildest reaches of Bitter Creek. The camera clicked and another tourist sat back exulting in the belief that he had the original and authentic picture of the West at its best—and its worst. One more picture of Topeka Totten would shortly adorn some remote album to be pointed at. This was fame.

So much was the usual ritual. But on this morning, the almost unusual happened. A coach door opened and a tall, slim man stepped down. Then the train slid on, the observation passed through and a woman lifted a white and graceful hand to murmur, "How picturesquely fascinating." The whistle of the engine cut off the rest. Distance absorbed the Transcontinental, leaving the tall man silent and thoughtful on the cindered platform.

The sharp eyes of the loungers dissected this stranger as a surgeon would have dissected a cadaver. He was about six feet and leather brown. He had a lean face molded into bold features. Yellow hair showed beneath the rim of his hat. Quiet gray eyes swept the little crowd with a lazy glance and passed on. In different clothing he would have answered as a man of the range country, but the fashionable suit he wore—which Topeka Totten mentally called "elegant and some nobby"—gave him away as an Eastern pilgrim with a spurious suntan.

It was a gray, pin-striped suit with vest and high lapels. There was a white collar and shirt, too, and a pair of low shoes that nobody around Crowheart would have worn to a dogfight. Just a good-looking dude who had made the error of stepping off at the wrong town.

This good looking dude was absorbing as well as being absorbed. He dropped his suitcase and rolled himself a cigarette, running his tongue along the edge in a manner dexterous enough to irritate the onlookers. How in hell could a dude build a smoke like that? Must be another one of those freaks who had read about Western ways and was trying to imitate them. When the cigarette was drawing evenly the man picked up his grip, walked by the group with a casual nod and rounded the station to confront the long strip of buildings across the way.

He stopped again, studying the town through half-closed eyes—the zigzag outline of the false fronts, the faded and peeling names on the boards—stable, hotel, mercantile emporiums, barber shop, court-house, hitching racks, watering troughs softly gur-gling, the Good Indian Saloon, the Crowheart Belle Saloon, Otto Ziegler's Resort. All this sprawling, loose-jointed town lay a-slumber in the fresh sun-light. A rider came along the dust, sitting high and easy and vital. Another man strolled from the hotel, stretching himself like a dog just risen. Swampers were sweeping the litter of a previous night out of the saloons to the sidewalk.

The strangers eyes flickered with a rising humor. He chuckled. Then his eyes caught a sign on a second story window: KIDDER, ATTORNEY AND J.P. As he saw it he moved forward, long fingers closing about the suitcase handle.

Once he had passed beyond earshot the half-dozen loungers moved in perfect unison toward the four big trunks dumped from the baggage coach to the waiting hand truck. Topeka Totten, being dean of Crowheart's men about town, solemnly took it upon himself to read aloud the labels attached to the trunks.

"Name's John France."

"Where from, Topeka?"

"Tag says Omaha." And Topeka tentatively hefted each trunk.

"Must be a drummer," suggested one.

But Topeka had not met trains all these years for nothing. "Uh-uh. He ain't fat like a drummer, and he wasn't smokin' no cigar. And if he was a drummer he'd of come right up to us and called us brother or old hoss or somethin' like that and talked like a greased hog goin' down a slippery chute."

"Kind of a scantlin' man."

"Them kind is deceivin'," stated Topeka. "Muscles is flat and plumb potent. Notice his hands? Brown as tobacco juice and long fingered. They've done seen labor."

"Prob'ly got brown from sittin' on the observation car," suggested another. "What in thunder does a man need four trunks for? I carry my belongin's in my pocket and ain't crowded none either."

"Uh-huh, I notice. If you had more maybe you'd borrow less."

"That so? Well, I borrow from men as has got something, Squint, which is why I ain't never hit you for nothin'."

"That's a bald-faced lie—"

Topeka had sidled away to command the town's street. "He's gone up to Kidder's. That means somethin'. Usual, a man goes to the hotel first." A gleam came to his eyes.

"Ain't no credit for him to be palaverin' with Kidder. Say, I wonder . . . ?"

They swapped speculative glances. A lawyer meant law. And law in the Crowheart country, as one-sided as it was, meant direct action. Again in unison the now highly interested half-dozen moseyed around the station, heading for the spot to which all news sooner or later came and from which a great deal of it started— Ziegler's Resort. But Topeka Totten split away from the group with a mysterious nod and planted himself on the edge of the hotel porch which flanked the stairway to Kidder's office.

"Which, I wonder?" he muttered. "Is it the fly goin' up to meet the spider, or two spiders talkin' things over in a friendly way? He didn't look Kidder's kind none."

The stranger, meanwhile, had gone up the stairs and let himself into a littered little room that looked a great deal like a rat's nest. Papers carpeted the floor. More papers, tied in bundles, were stacked along the corners. An old roll-top desk with its countless pigeonholes bulging with letters, legal forms, cartridge

11

boxes, brand marks and assorted hardware stood in the center of this room. And before the roll-top desk sat a stub of a man sheathed in successive layers of fat; a man with distended, yellow jowls and beaming little pig eyes; a man who held a pen in a hand so puffed with tissue that the fingers seemed nothing but stubs. This was Kidder, Attorney and J.P.

Kidder scratched a slightly scrofulous neck with the end of the pen and looked around at the newcomer.

"G'mornin'," he said. "Deposition, legal advice, real estate, general information? Entirely at your service, Mister—I didn't catch the name."

The stranger smiled, brushed a stack of dusty books from the only vacant chair and sat himself down. Still smiling, he pulled various letters and official appearing forms from his pocket and casually dropped them on Kidder's desk.

"The name," he drawled, "is John France."

Something happened inside Kidder that set his jowls to quivering like mounds of jelly. The small eyes riveted themselves on the stranger, stuck there fascinated a moment, and dropped to the papers before him. The puffy fingers went to pawing through them. Sundry grunting noises emerged from Kidder's throat and then one hand dived into an open drawer and came out with several chocolates that described a brief arc and disappeared in Kidder's little bud of a mouth. Thus gurgling over the chocolates this lawyer alternately read and thrust sidling glances at John France. At each inspection a different expression passed over lawyer

Kidder's fat face, and finally, the chocolates gone and the reading done, he leaned back in the chair and folded his hands across the rounding vat that was his stomach.

"So you're the nevvy of old Ike France, deceased," he muttered, "and come to take over the ranch he willed you. Now that is sad. Hate to see a pilgrim come to the country and get all busted up. I will say no more."

"Is the climate bad?" drawled John France, inspecting Kidder with a half-lidded glance.

"Fine climate, best in the world," the lawyer assured him.

"Somebody else contesting my right to the ranch?"

"Not a soul."

"Then what is so bad about my inheriting this property?"

"I will say no more," repeated Kidder and reached for additional chocolates.

"Seems like a peaceful country."

"Appearances," said Kidder in his heaviest manner, "don't cut no ice with the true facts. Where you from, anyhow?"

"Points east and south."

"Ever run a ranch before, Mr. France?"

"No-o, can't exactly say that."

"Know much about cattle?"

"Guess I could draw a picture of one from memory." France grinned.

Kidder nodded. "It's about what I thought. No

13

stranger to the country can ever expect to cut the mustard, friend. Runnin' an outfit is tough business, even for an old head. You got a lot of grief comin'. What I expected. Well, Ike's been dead six months. I ain't the administrator of the estate. Ike didn't see fit to make me that. He left it to that Omaha bank, which commissioned me to take care of things while they rustled up remainin' heirs. Personal, I didn't figure Ike had any heirs, remote or otherwise. Guess that bank had a hard job locatin' you, huh?"

"It was news to me. Never knew anything about the old duck. Never knew he had a ranch. Never saw him in my life. He was a different branch of the family. Well, I expect my credentials are good enough for you, Kidder?"

France thought Kidder's nod was a little bit reluctant so he asked a few more questions.

"Where is the ranch?"

"Ten miles due north from town."

"How much beef is it carrying?"

Kidder shook his head. He was distinctly on guard. "Wouldn't guarantee to say. Never knew nothin' about Ike's business in the first place and I don't know what's happened since. The Omaha bank told me to keep some sort of crew workin' on the place while they found next of kin to take charge. That's all I done. I been keepin' five men on the premises." Kidder's eyes flitted across France and away. "Of course, you understand I ain't responsible. Ike's original crew quit when he died and I been havin' difficulties gettin' men to work there. Had to take what I could get. Maybe it's a little run down. Things like that happen."

"Uh-huh," France agreed and rolled another cigarette. By and by he shot another question at the lawyer. "What did my uncle Ike die of?"

Kidder's yeasty body moved in the chair. "Some sort of complications. Don't exactly know. Took him off sudden-like."

France's manner was calm yet somehow insistent. "Any marks of violence?"

At that Kidder lifted his puffy hands, palms up. "I wasn't goin' to say much about that for fear of hurtin' your family pride. It ain't a nice thing. Old Ike was in poor health a long spell. We found him out on the range, lyin' on his face. Bullet through his heart. Plain case of despondent suicide."

"Who said it was a plain case?"

Kidder's manner became somewhat truculent. "Look here, you're talkin' like a prosecutor. I should think a pilgrim would accept the plain word of an old-timer in the country. It was the coroner's verdict, Mr. France."

"We'll consider the matter closed, then," France decided, grinding the cigarette beneath a boot heel. "At least until something comes up to unsettle that belief."

"What you mean by such a statement?" Kidder said.

France rose, shaking his head. "Nothing important. I'll expect you to introduce me over at the bank and to the folks around here in general. Meanwhile I'm going to wash up at the hotel and get a bite. Also arrange for a team to take me and my forty year's gathering out to the place. What's the brand mark of my outfit?"

"Main brand is Circle IF. You got two others, the 77 and the Double Diamond."

France nodded and left the office with a brief, "See you later." Lawyer Kidder waited until he heard the man's footsteps die from the stairway and then hauled himself out of the chair and put his head through the open window. France was just then entering the hotel. Kidder turned and took to the stairs with an alacrity that set him to wheezing like an engine. On the street he swung past the hotel and stopped at Ziegler's Resort. A little later a messenger left Ziegler's and hurried to the courthouse. Presently a third man hurried from the courthouse, struggling into his coat. A star flashed momentarily in the sunlight and was concealed.

This individual stepped inside Ziegler's a brief moment and, using the back door, went to the stable. Still later he was riding east from Crowheart. Three miles down the tracks he brought up before an outfit driving cattle through a series of chutes into livestock cars set on the siding. A conference here resulted in a puncher leaving the work and racing north over the uneven plain toward the spires of an encircling mountain range. The messenger from Crowheart, who was Sheriff Poco Finn, returned to town with a gentleman by the name of Crossjack Drood.

## CHAPTER II

Unmindful of this swift movement of antagonistic elements, John France slicked himself in the hotel room, extracted a few objects from his suitcase and stowed them around his pockets. After that he went down, augured a late breakfast from an unwilling waitress and presently had her smiling favorably at him. The breakfast was ample and he did full justice to it in spite of the fact that he already had eaten on the train. There was something in this prairie air that set up a man's appetite and made him eager to be moving, to be in the saddle and questing the rolling miles that led toward the fresh, snow-tipped spire points. All the way from Omaha, John France had looked forward to what he was about to find, but the country surprised him with its heady air, its mist-blue and velvet-brown reaches. It was more than he had expected and the eagerness within him increased.

Leaving the hotel, he observed that Crowheart was no longer sleepy, no longer half-emptied of life. Quite a number of men loafed along the street with no particular errand seeming to bother them. Ziegler's Resort, he further observed, was doing considerable business. A pair of riders galloped by, looking fully at him, and the rest of the citizens were giving him a measured if covert appraisal. John France chuckled to himself and entered the stable.

He arranged for a flatbed wagon and a team, turned to go and was halted on the sidewalk by the drum of an approaching cavalcade. Half a dozen horsemen swung in from the town's west end and pounded past the stable at a full gallop. He heard a voice, one that certainly wasn't a man's, explaining something, and then the group came to a swirling halt in front of the hotel and a lithe figure dropped to the ground and walked up to the porch. John France lost interest in all else.

It was a girl dressed in riding cords and boots. A flame colored neckpiece fluttered about her throat. A white hand reached impatiently for a Stetson and revealed a mass of auburn hair that caught the sun's brightness and shimmered with an astonishing radiance. The group with her seemed to be arguing about something, and she turned from the hotel doorway to stop the argument in a cool and abrupt voice that carried over to France.

"Now cut this debate and get going," she said. "We haven't any time to waste. And if any of you boys try to blot up Ziegler's kegs I'll skin you."

For a moment she watched them, a level and unshaken confidence in every line of her graceful body. Almost an arrogant sureness. Then she disappeared inside the hotel.

France gave his attention to the saloons, the humor leaving his gray eyes. "There's a whole lot I don't know about this country," he told himself, "and I expect I'll get some surprises before I'm much older.

It's too much to expect of human nature—about that ranch. I'd better announce myself right off and get it over with."

To Zieglers he swung, judging that saloon to be the most favored rendezvous in town.

Meanwhile, two men had gone into the courthouse and around to the sheriff's office. These men were Crossjack Drood, powerful rancher, and Poco Finn, sheriff of the county. The sheriff sat down and hung his feet on the desk with the air of a man who, having well performed a duty, felt the need of rest.

"I figured you'd want to know," he said, "which is why I come right away to tell you. He sashays into Kidder's office, flashes his identification papers and says he's the sole heir of old Ike's ranch. Kidder came to me the first chance he got. Guess you never figured on any heir, did you? Never heard Ike speak of any kith or kin."

Drood tramped an endless circle, his swart and heavy-boned head swung forward on an eighteen-inch neck. At fifty, this man showed neither white hair nor diminution of energy. In the surrounding country he was the hardest worker, the most insistent driver of men. Tireless, acquisitive, and without a shred of humor, he reached out for the only things he ever cared about—money and power.

"A pilgrim, was he?"

"Well, Kidder said he talked like one and still he didn't. Wears Eastern clothes. Don't look dangerous."

"Credentials all right? No chance to contest 'em?"

19

"Kidder says not."

"Damn Kidder! No matter what that fat tub of butter says, this fellow has got to be stopped in his tracks. Greenhorn or old head, he's dangerous either way. It's too late in the day for any of us to be interfered with. Especially right at this time of the year. We've had no warning. He can find enough evidence around the range to hang the bunch. Is—"

Another man slipped through the office—a lank, sorrel creature with slate eyes and a hatchet chin. This was Big Dan Golloway, by trade a gunfighter. "Saw you come here,' he said. "Talkin' about that stranger?"

Drood pulled his head up. "He's come to take over Ike's ranch, Dan."

"Mebbe the takin' will be too big a job for him. You worryin'?"

"The time to stop him is right now, boys. Dan, you—"

"Oh, yeah. Me. So I got to do some chore again? Why not you or Poco, or maybe our friend—"

Drood broke through impatiently. "You go over and find him. Pick a quarrel with him. Put the fear of God in his heart and tell him when the next train leaves. No shootin'. Just rough him up. He's an Easterner and he'll cave in."

"Shucks, why have I got to—"

"Listen," Drood said angrily, "if he ever gets near that ranch we're all fit subjects for the pen. The gate is wide open. Get it, Golloway? Our tracks is plenty and plain for him to see. You start movin'."

20

The third man ruminated a bit, then nodded his head slowly and went out.

John France's passage into Ziegler's Resort seemed to establish a suction that drew others casually behind him. The stale odors of the previous night had hardly gone from the vast room, yet a considerable crowd lounged around the tables and at the bar. Immediately he was the focus of all eyes and he felt that in with the curiosity there was also a mixture of veiled hostility. He had seen men look like that before. But, ignoring the attention with an even gravity, he walked toward the bar. Right beside him a pair of men were engaged in a jangling, acrimonious argument. One of them was accusing the other in severe language, and that other, whom France recognized as one of the station loiterers, was feebly defending himself.

"You're so drunk, you drip," said the accuser, waving a finger. "Topeka, damn your miserable hide, can't I turn around without you hit for a saloon like a shot duck? You're drunk."

"Slim, I ain't had more'n a drop."

"You're drunk!"

"I ain't!"

"No? Well, I'll dang soon find out. Stand up straight, put your heels together. Now say it. And if you miss a syllable I'll wring that dog poison out of you with my bare hands."

Topeka Totten clicked his heels and blew an aromatic breath. A glassy stare came to his eyes and he gulped. Like some overgrown lunkhead of a schoolboy he recited: "Swift sailed the swallow shell over the swelling sea while the Mississippi lisped lissomely on the slipping, shallow lea."

"I guess you ain't drunk,' admitted the accuser grudgingly.

Topeka swelled with a justifiable pride. He hadn't expected to say it himself. "Doggone your ornery soul, Slim Hillis, you owe me a drink."

"Have one on me," was John France's quiet interjection. Then he lifted his voice. "Everybody up to have a snort. This is going to be a dry day."

The crowd knew its etiquette and its inclination. It advanced forthwith to the bar. A spry little man in broadcloth came around to serve France personally. "My name's Ziegler. I run this dump. I never allow a pilgrim to buy his first drink in my place. It's on the house. Here's mud in your eye, friend."

"Thank you kindly," said France, and manfully absorbed the punishment. Slim Hillis took his jolt at a swallow. When his breath came back he yodeled a high note and tried to tear the mahogany bar in half. Then, catching hold of himself, he cast a sober glance at Ziegler.

"I dunno as that is a friendly wish to the stranger, Otto."

"Why not?" snapped Ziegler.

Slim Hillis stiffened his five-feet-nine inches and looked to the taller John France. He was a blue-eyed man, this Hillis, and latent deviltry peeped out. In a crowd of more or less tall and husky individuals he looked far from dangerous. Yet there was a worldly wisdom on his homely face and he carried himself with a free and easy assurance. For some unexplained reason France found he was swapping grins with Hillis.

"Why not?" repeated Ziegler, studying the puncher unpleasantly.

Hillis shrugged his shoulders and spoke with an exaggerated drawl. "Why, I wouldn't wish mud in nobody's eye in a country which is infested with people that got the habit of pot-shootin' other folks from off angles."

"Tryin' to give this stranger a bad impression of Crowheart, huh?" Ziegler spat behind him, conveying an expressive contempt for such treason. "You always was a herd jumper, Hillis. Can't string along with a decent bunch more than ten minutes without wantin' to take a bite out of somebody's flanks. If this country don't suit you, why in hell do you stay?"

"I'm stickin' around to see a few gents die," was the puncher's even answer.

"And who might they be?" challenged Ziegler, placing both hands on the bar and staring at Hillis.

"If the shoe fits, Otto," said Hillis very softly, "put it on."

Ziegler was no coward, but after a steady appraisal of the puncher's bland face he lifted his shoulders and contented himself with saying, "One of these days somebody's goin' to call you for loose remarks like that."

23

France casually intervened. "I haven't bought that drink yet. My turn now. Everybody liquidate on a new citizen in Crowheart, meaning self. Though you have probably been already notified by the usual grapevine route, my name is France and I expect to run the Circle IF."

He poured his own whiskey and lifted the glass. But he never drank that jolt. A sorrel, slab-sided fellow as tall as any man in the room crowded Hillis aside and struck France's elbow so hard that glass and contents fell on the bar. In the snapping of a finger all talk quit, the bar was cleared of drinkers, and a wide lane sprang into existence. France turned to find a hatchet face set near his own and a slaty, sullen glare striking him belligerently.

"My mistake, maybe," drawled France. "If it's room you want I'll move over some."

"I ain't apologizin'," grunted hatchet face. "Why in hell don't you keep your elbows down? Seems like all you Eastern dudes put on a lot of airs around plain folks."

"I didn't catch the name," France murmured.

"Big Dan Golloway, fella. You'll catch more of it providin' you stay around here long. Which I doubt."

"Well, let's christen the beginning of a great friendship with appropriate fluid."

"I ain't drinkin' with dudes, and I ain't drinkin' with you."

The silence held a painful tension. Glancing around, John France saw half a hundred curious eyes watching him. Slim Hillis looked on without a vestige of personal interest, as graven-faced as if he were studying a straight flush before the draw. Otto Ziegler had moved away from the bar and was mechanically polishing a glass, never turning his attention toward France. This was the way cattle country sat in on trouble.

"What seems to be bitin' you?" France wanted to know, a little sing-song melody playing through the words. His head tipped forward and the gray eyes were as mild as spring.

I don't like your face," snapped Golloway. "It ain't built right. I don't like dude clothes, I don't like dudes and specially I don't like your kind of a dude. Sink your teeth in that, kid."

"The clothes won't bother you much longer, Golloway," drawled France. "But the face is plumb permanent. We'll have to do something about this. Far be it from me to give suffering to one of Crowheart's prominent citizens."

"We'll do somethin' about it all right," growled Golloway. "If I see it around here much longer I'll change it. They's a train goin' East this afternoon."

"Speaking of faces," observed France, "yours looks crooked to me. Is that just an idle fancy of mine or am I right?"

"Shut up, you yella-striped beanpole!"

.France moved imperceptibly, a piece of a smile turning up the corners of his mouth. "Well, my lad, this has been good clean fun up to now, but the party's

25

getting rough. I'm a moral man and I strive to please. If you've been looking for something, here it comes."

His right fist moved up from his belt. The solid impact smacked into the four-cornered silence of the place. Big Dan Golloway's hat flew off and his chin skewed back. He made a grab for the bar, missed it and fell flat on his spine. The crowd sprang farther away. Otto Ziegler sank below the bar with a dignified astonishment on his face. Then Golloway rolled over and rose up, reaching for his belt. Both hands froze there. This guileless pilgrim from the East had reached into the thin air and snapped a gun. The traffic end of it yawned abysmally on Golloway. France was speaking again.

"I expected sooner or later to have somebody force my hand, but I didn't think it would come before my breakfast had settled. I don't know what you've got on your chest, dog bait, but if you cough good and hearty it will probably disappear. If this is your own bright idea just get it out of your head. I'm here to stay. If it's somebody else that pushed you into this manufactured scrap, go back and tell 'em I don't bluff easy. Now crawl out."

"Where'd you git that gun?" demanded Golloway.

"From a tougher egg than you. Push your feet out of here."

"I'll make you eat that thing before I'm finished!" bawled Golloway. "I'll bust every bone in your body. No Eastern sucker can make a fool out of me that-away!"

"Pretty hard to improve on the original article. Now scat!"

Golloway's thin nose was white down to the distended nostrils. Swollen veins tinged the balls of his eyes. But he swung wide of France and tramped doggedly out of Ziegler's Resort without another word. Men began to talk in nervous spurts. Slim Hillis rolled a cigarette and a broad, pleased grin spread from ear to ear.

"Otto," said France to the still crouching Ziegler, "you can come up for air. How much do I owe you?"

Ziegler straightened, displeased and gruff. "Don't get proud over that play. You got an unfair drop on Big Dan. People that come to Crowheart had oughta stick to their own business. You got no call gettin' hard nosed."

"That's right. I want to know where I stand. Am I to take it you're on Golloway's side of the bobwire?"

That's my business!" snapped Ziegler.

"Also correct," agreed France, leaning forward. The next words were far less friendly. "But it is only correct as long as you keep it your business and don't meddle with anybody else's."

The doors swung open and a freckle-faced cowhand waddled over to France. "Laurel Annison wants to see you," said he abruptly. "Right away."

It had the sound of a summons to the royal presence. France smiled down on the puncher and shook his head. "Please give the lady my regrets and say I have a previous engagement for about fifteen minutes."

"Sa-ay, it's Laurel Annison that's tellin' you to come."

"Be sure and give her my regrets," repeated France. "I'll be there in about fifteen minutes."

"I'll be dummed," the puncher said and went out, highly affronted. "Sayin' that to Laurel Annison!"

## CHAPTER III

Slim Hillis turned to Topeka Totten. "You and me are takin' a powder and passin' out. Come on."

But Topeka, who had a greedy ear for news, was reluctant to pass up so many splendid possibilities. Within the shiftless, whiskey-soaked body was a hard streak of wisdom. He understood sooner than any other man in Crowheart that from now on all events centered around the tall and deceptively mild John France, and he wanted to warm his inquisitive soul in the reflected glow of this man who so casually focused the intrigue and the violence of Crowheart's most powerful ring.

"Let's stay a little bit longer, Slim," he muttered. "Somethin's goin' to happen here. Hell, he ain't no more pilgrim than me or you. A pilgrim would walk out. He knows better. He's stickin' around to give 'em a chance to come back."

"We're goin'," was Slims retort. "We got business outside. I like that fella and I aim to constitute myself an ace in the hole."

"Oh, well," Topeka said, and went.

John France paid his bill to the suddenly taciturn Otto Ziegler, then hooked his elbows against the bar in a manner to command both the front and rear doors of the saloon—and at that point everybody in the place ceased to regard him as a pilgrim. This was the move of an old hand. Still aloof, the crowd watched him with hawklike interest for a sign of nervousness.

There was none. At the end of a quarter-hour, still serene and lazy, he gave up his post and sauntered from Ziegler's. The fresh sunlight fell in his eyes and for a moment he paused to get his bearings, looking right and left. Here and there a townsman moved. Slim Hillis and Topeka Totten squatted on the sidewalk edge fifty feet away, absorbed in their own palaver. Big Dan Golloway was not to be seen. Crossing to the stable, he found his wagon and team ready. He drove out and around to the station, there taking his trunks aboard. Wheeling back to the hotel, he tied the reins on the brake handle and went up for his suitcase.

Observing this from afar, Topeka Totten nodded his head. "Can't tell me that man's a pilgrim, Slim. Just the way he wrops them ribbons around the brake handle augurs xperience."

Might," grunted Slim Hillis and was moved to a puzzled wonder. "Topeka, I plumb don't understand how a man that's got as much gray matter and sharp sense as you have got can be so damn no-account otherwise."

29

Topeka's seamy face settled. He looked straight ahead of him, into the dim haze of his past. "I was pretty good in my time, Slim. Don't look it, but I owned a ranch and had a family. I signed my name to checks and I killed my rustlers. Somewhere in Texas is a town"—this came out of him in reluctant sadness—"which is named after me. But the left hand road is an easy one, amigo. I took it. All I got to do now is die like a gentleman."

"How about that family?" Slim inquired gruffly. He never would have presumed to ask the question had not Topeka been a friend over years of time. The man had never before opened up like this.

"Dead," droned Topeka, and then without shifting his eyes or raising his voice he added, "Dan Golloway just rode around the back end of the courthouse. He's cuttin' east and north from town."

"Drood and Poco Finn are still in the courthouse," said Slim. "Well, I be boiled in mutton fat! There's Louise Drood crossin' to the hotel."

A girl in denim overalls came out of a drygoods store and walked swiftly to the hotel porch. She sat down in a chair near the steps, her jet black hair bobbing forward and the white triangle of her throat gleaming against a man's dark shirt.

"Looks to me like that gang is stoopin' to a dirty kind of frameup," Topeka said.

"Don't bank on Louise too much. She don't track with her daddy all the time. Listen, you stick to town and keep that elephant ear of yours close to the ground. I'm dealin' myself a hand in this little game. France may invite me to run my nose up another alley but I'm takin' the chance."

"Hop to," was Topeka's laconic answer, seemingly buried in his own sorrows. But there was nothing on that street he failed to pick up. Slim Hillis strolled casually to the stable and later rode from town.

When John France came out of the hotel with his suitcase he found himself halted in his tracks by a pair of intensely black and inviting eyes. There was nothing reticent about Louise Drood. When this tempestuous, full-bosomed girl wanted a thing she went after it with an appalling directness. For one instant she regarded France, and in that instant she knew all she wanted to know and for the rest of her life could have described every line and shifting emotion of his face. Her dark head bobbed a little and cherry-red lips parted in a flashing smile.

"Hello."

France reached for his hat, smiling back. "Hello."

"You don't know me. I'm Louise Drood."

"I'm handsomely pleased. My name is—"

"John France," interrupted the girl, rising with a sudden impatience. Even in overalls and rough shirt she made a vivid picture. "I know all about you. This dinky town is a regular women's sewing circle for gossip. You're taking over old Ike's Circle IF. When I heard it I wanted to know what kind of a fool would ever buck that. That's why I'm sitting here."

"Found out, I reckon," drawled France, inwardly

uncertain of his ground. Direct attack from a woman was something he had never been trained to cope with.

She had a swift gesture of hand and shoulder for that. "I think you'll be able to take care of yourself. I want to see you again, John France. Don't forget, Drood's ranchhouse is eight miles north of your back door as the crow flies. I can tell you right now my dad won't like you, but that doesn't cut any ice with me. I'll be the reception committee. How's that?"

"Sounds slick," agreed France.

She studied him more closely and the direct, sure frankness was clouded by a wistful attempt to be candid with him. "I've been called a siren, but did you ever hear of a siren wearing overalls and going hell-bent for election on a horse?"

"Don't believe I ever have," said France, and then snapped his fingers in irritation. "Now that reminds me I was supposed to meet a lady. Clean forgot it. Who is Laurel Annison?"

"Oh, Laurel. So she crooked her finger at you right away?" The girl's lips curled into sulky lines. "She traveled out of here ten minutes ago lookin' like she wanted to bite somebody. So you kept her waiting, did you? Let me tell you something—you'll pay for that."

France grinned. "Maybe I'd better keep out of her way."

"You can't if she won't let you," stated the girl. "Well, don't forget you've got a standing invitation to the Drood's hacienda."

"I'm obliged," said France and climbed to the wagon seat. Louise Drood watched out of her dark eyes, swept him up and down, and was smiling when he turned to lift his hat again. So she stood until the wagon tooled along the street and swung left with the road as it began undulating north to the spire points. Then she dropped her eyes to the rough clothes she wore and grew suddenly stormy.

"I've lived around men so long I look like one! I'm just a slouchy kid and he didn't give me a second look! Well, I'll change that in a hurry."

Back to the drygoods store she went, and there she remained until her father's rough summons drew her out.

"What you doin' in town again, Louise? Buyin'. Always buyin' somethin'. And I thought I told you to leave that claybank alone. I ain't goin' to have you bustin' into my string. Get into the leather. I'm takin' a quick trip home."

She obeyed and, with her elbows cramped with packages, rode north alongside the silent Crossjack Drood. They passed John France without a word. Louise didn't as much as glance at the man she had previously introduced herself to. She knew better than that; for this man was her father's enemy even though the two of them had never met. She knew all about her father's business, and until now it had never worried her. But as they cantered forward little furrows of thought deepened into the white forehead and her eyes pooled up a troubled wistfulness.

· · ·

A great country. That was John France's increasingly delightful conviction. The spring air contained a tonic that carried right through a man's skin and made him want to step high. Recent rains had softened the earth to unlock root and seed from the iron grip of winter. A warming, brilliant sun flashed through the immeasurable blue canopy to touch off the primal impulse of birth and growth. He could almost feel the ferment of the upspringing grasses, while the damp incense of soil and vegetation touched his lungs at every breath.

Ahead and beside him the prairie swelled, dipped and swelled again as it rose to bench and from bench to ridge. Left and right at no great distance, these ridges paralleled him and sidled gradually inward until they met and formed a country that rolled into high parks, water-washed holes and snow pointed peaks. The pines yonder were emerald green, the skyline cut sharply against a transparent distance. Straggling groups of cattle ranged here and there. A horseman topped a not far removed roll and poised like a statue. It was good to be alive.

"The folks said Ike was a fool to cut loose and come to this country," he reflected. "I wonder now who was foolish? My notion of something slick is to stick right here until the sod takes me. That may be distant or it may be near, according to the brand of politics played around these parts. But this ranch isn't going to be handed to me on a platter. So much is plenty clear."

France wasn't blind and he wasn't green. He could

see that Crowheart didn't expect him and didn't welcome him. Even though he had been in the town a few hours he had felt a cloud of sullen opposition crawl around him, thick enough to be cut with a meat cleaver. The lawyer was either dishonest or afraid. That Golloway jasper set a tune right off, and the bulk of the townsmen seemed to take their cue from him.

"Where honey is the bees will gather," he thought. "There's a ranch all stocked and lying ownerless for half a year. What would be apt to happen? You guessed right the first time, Johnny. Bright boy. And again, maybe not so bright. Golloway, unless I'm the left-handed son of a left-handed prophet, tried to haze me out of the pasture before I even lifted a hoof to get in. And if they don't want me to get possession, how in the name of thunder do I figure to keep going after I do hang up my war bag in Circle IF? I don't know anybody, I've got no friends to draw from, and I can't tell who I should trust. No, Johnny, not so bright. Just too stubborn to have good sense. Which reminds me, I forgot to have that hulk of a lawyer write me an introduction to the hands on the place. So I've got to establish myself. And here comes somebody."

A rider swelled up from an arroyo and bore down, molded to the saddle with reckless easy grace. The man began to look familiar and presently he recognized Slim Hillis from the peculiar point of the latter's shoulders. Hillis wanted a talk, that was clear; so France dragged the ribbons and waited. Hillis came up with a round turn that put his artillery on the far side, grinning amiably.

"Anyhow," he drawled, "the weather around Crow-heart is good."

France, drawn by the smaller man's casual, humorous self-confidence, matched the grin. "Man doesn't have to go far to put himself out of sight," he observed. "Another good item."

Hillis chuckled. "Straight to the button, huh? Yeah, I did pop up sort of sudden. But I didn't want Cross-jack Drood to see me."

"So? That was the girl's daddy that went by with her? Friendly cuss."

"Friendly as two broken legs. You see, I'm a sort of moral leper around here. A little Orphant Annie that can't find no washin' to take in. Who am I to intrude myself on Mr. Crossjack Drood's presence?"

"So?" murmured France and studied Slim Hillis with a long, steady regard. The man's blue eyes matched the glance inscrutably. "Not much work for a man around here, then? Outfits all full up."

"Depends," grunted Hillis. "Not much work for me less I tackle Laurel Annison's outfit. Laurel's a good kid but I chew and drink and I even swear. And I don't like a woman boss."

"I understand," mused France, "that my outfit has got a few riders already." He kept his attention on Slim Hillis' face, watching for shifts of expression. Hillis only said, "Yeah, you got some men. Four-five. Circle IF carried fifteen hands once."

36

France decided he knew his man right there. Slim Hillis was not talking out of turn but in the slow matter of fact answers dwelt a suggestive inflection. So Circle IF's new owner reached for his wheat papers and shot a direct question at Hillis.

"How'd you like to be Number One on my outfit?"

Hillis shook his head. "Not with the boys already there. I never sent a Christmas card to any of 'em, and I think they might hold it against me."

"So I judged," was France's comment. "It was in my head you could probably pick up a half-dozen boys to take their place. There's an old sayin' about a new broom sweepin' clean."

"Yeah, if you can get the damn thing to sweep at all," was the man's pointed reply. "I don't gossip, France, but since you made me the offer I will observe it might be difficult to fire that bunch."

"I'll take the chance," drawled France. "Offer still stands."

"You know what you're up against?" demanded Hillis.

"I sort of thought," reflected France, "you might be able to round up about six boys who wouldn't wilt on the stem. The kind that would be good to their parents but sort of weaned from the Santy Claus idea."

Suddenly Hillis slapped his thigh, chuckling. "I knew damn well you wasn't no pilgrim. Don't know where you come from, but you talk my language. I'll be at the Circle IF in the morning with my bunch. Take me a lot of ridin' to get 'em, but you believe me

37

they'll be up to snuff. I doubt if any of 'em has got parents. They're hard to look at, and they're a little bit wild. Don't worry about it—they'll mind me."

"Leave it to you," agreed France, gathering the ribbons.

Hillis was searching around to express an awkward sentiment. "You don't know me from Adam's off ox. How come you trust me this way?"

"Had a partner in Colorado that looked like you one time," drawled France. "I know the earmarks."

"Uh-huh. Well, you won't be sorry. By the way, there's a dip in the trail two miles ahead. It passes between high walls. Was I you I'd circle around. Rock might slide down and crush your hat."

"Good idea," said France. "See you in the morning."

He put the team in motion and rolled on up the slant of the prairie. When he looked around, Slim Hillis was pounding down the road to Crowheart, a faint dust marking his speed. France nodded.

"It's a gamble, but I think I guessed right. Sure cinch I've got to take some chances if I expect to weather through the next few weeks. He knows the country and everybody in it. But he wouldn't open his mouth to me unless he was working for the outfit. What was that he said about Drood?"

Presently, two miles onward and four hundred feet higher, he reached the flanking walls of a rocky butte. The road dived between the butte and the high country to his right but France stopped a moment to study the rim of the walls and the country to either side. A rough detour was available if he wanted to go around, but it meant a loss of time and—which was more important to him—it meant a loss of self-confidence. If he ever expected to survive in this country he had to brace things boldly. So he crawled back to the wagon bed, opened a trunk and took out a rifle and a box of shells. Throwing cartridges into the magazine, he laid the gun on the seat beside him and went ahead.

Nothing happened. Beyond the butte the open prairie closed quickly into the broken country. The road's grade stiffened and took to curving left and right. Left and right also the ridges came closer, and a river's shallow surface sparkled brilliantly across the distance.

An hour later he drove the team through a long, rising pass and came into a broad mountain meadow. At the far end were a low log house and outbuildings and corrals. Smoke spiraled from a chimney, and a creek came charging down from the surrounding peaks.

Nowhere in his traveled years had John France ever set foot upon a more desirable stretch of ground. High above the world it rested, remote and self-contained, a pleasant place in which to live. He knew it was Circle IF because of the brand burned into a post of the main gate. Reaching out from the wagon seat he hauled down a rope and draw bar, waited for the gate to swing before him, and passed through. And as he pulled up before the main house he saw that the double set of footprints he had followed all along the road—made by Drood and the girl—also drew in here.

At first he figured the place deserted. Then a dragging step echoed through an open door and a wide-girthed man appeared and slouched against a porch post. A jet and curly beard lay along a triangular face. Smoke-colored eyes, deeply set in the rounding bone, sullenly met and challenged him.

"Circle IF, I reckon?" drawled France.

"The truth," grunted the man.

"My name's France."

"You said it," said the fellow, as if he refused to believe what he heard. France smiled, yet a quick pressure pinched in his lips.

"I've come to take over the outfit," France said and climbed from the seat. There was a moment's pause, broken by a sarcastic phrase from the bearded one.

"Expect me to swallow that story hide, hair and teeth, huh? Mister, lots of tricks have been worked on us boys, and we ain't exactly green. We take orders from Kidder in Crowheart. Where's he at?"

"Pays to be careful," admitted France and reached for his credentials. "Lay your eyes on that and you'll feel better."

The man never lifted his arms. "We take orders from Kidder," was his surly answer.

"All right. That's fair enough. I'll see you get orders from Kidder. Meanwhile I'm moving in."

France casually unloaded his trunks, boosted them to the porch, picked up his grip and started for the door. The man blocked it. "Don't be in no hurry,

Mister. You get Kidder up here first."

France set the grip on the floor and considered this unfriendly custodian with a level gaze. "Pretty particular who comes around here I take it?"

"You bet."

"But not so particular about the visitors you had a little while ago?"

That touched the fellow. He straightened. He scowled. "That ain't any of your business, is it? How'd you know? When you're as well known in these parts as—" He paused and shrugged his shoulders. "I guess you better go get Kidder."

"In due time. Meanwhile you've got company. Move aside, friend."

"You tryin' to force my hand?" asked the fellow, bearing down on the words.

France stepped back a pace. "Caution, my friend, is one thing. Being impolite is another. You know better. I offered you some means of identification, which you didn't want to look at. Drood's been here, and he heard enough in town to be able to pass on the news, which he probably did. That ought to be some help to you. Also, it never was considered very friendly in my country to refuse a visitor shelter. I ain't as green as I look. I've had trouble already this morning, and I'm getting tired of it. If it's any help to your mind I'll say you're playing the wrong game. Step aside."

The man's smoky eyes dilated and went roving around France's body as if looking for a gun. Whatever he found or failed to find, he did not change his

41

tactics. He moved clear of the door and said nothing. France passed through and stood in a broad room littered and scarred by careless use. Dishes clattered beyond a wall and the smell of food sifted out; a fire flickered in a great stone hearth; stale tobacco smoke and whisky fumes clung to the place. The caretakers had lived well. Beside the fireplace, another door led into a bedroom. This, he found, was filthy with dirt and being used by one of the party. But he went in, closed the door and changed his clothes thoughtfully.

"They've got word," he said to himself. "Now who told them? Drood or somebody else? Don't make much difference. The point is I guess I've got to bear down on these buzzards without delay. Matter of example. If I hedge they'll think I'm no force and they'll spread the idea. Looks like I've been willed a bunch of grief."

Soon the Eastern clothes lay discarded on a chair and with them passed John France, pilgrim. Out of the grip came a faded, well-worn suit like ten thousand others in cattle land, scuffed boots with mark of spurs deeply channeled in them, and a Stetson that most apparently had fanned many fires and dipped much water. When he had this rig on him the mark of his calling could no longer be suppressed. Every inch of that tall and whipcord body was range grown, range seasoned. The bronze outline of his face, the sun-blackened and calloused hands, the lazy manner of carrying himself—all these were the unmistakable copyrights of a Western man.

Well, I'm out of that damn civilized harness and glad of it," he thought. "Cost me sixty dollars for a week's wear and made me feel like a barbershop pole."

France buckled a cartridge belt around him, took his gun from the bed and broke the chamber. For a short period he spun the cylinder with sober attention, then snapped it home and dropped the weapon into its holster seat. Well," he murmured, dropped days. I may be able to swing this and I may not. Here goes." Leaving the bedroom he walked back to the porch, to find the scene somewhat changed.

His trunks were piled back in the wagon, the wagon and team turned about and pointing south toward Crowheart. Below the steps of the porch stood five men, tall and short, slim and heavy, yet all alike in the guarded hostility of their eyes. A Chinese cook stood slightly aside from them, aproned and clutching a bread knife, and it was the Oriental who made the first overt move. His slanting orbs played over the tall, slim figure on the porch and then he walked from the group back to his kitchen with a mutter of weird words in his throat.

A lithe, girl-faced member of the group chuckled maliciously. "Well, well, Alfonso Aloysius Adelbert has gone and went and got himself some real clothes, just like the rude cowboy wears. Do I see hardware restin' on his stifle? I do. Ain't it pretty? Now I awsk you."

The bearded one intervened. "Shut up, Gib. You talk too much." Then he swung a fist at France. "It's our

43

opinion you'd do better back in Crowheart. Climb aboard."

"So sorry," mimicked the irrepressible Gib. "But you done went and forgot a previous engagement."

"Shut up, Gib!' There was a furrow of worry on the bearded one's forehead. The rest of the group looked on, weighing France detail by detail. This was not the same stranger at all.

"I thought," drawled France, "I put my trunks on the porch."

"We put 'em back," stated the spokesman. "Get goin'. We ain't fallin' for any slick tricks."

"Who told you to give me the razmataz?" inquired France.

"Better man than you," snorted Gib.

"Shut up, Gib, or I'll crack your mug wide open!" shouted the spokesman. "France—if that's your mon-icker, which I doubt—get aboard and travel."

"Pretty heavy trunks," opined France. "You bought yourself some extra labor. Just pull 'em right back off that wagon and tote 'em to my room."

"Like hell."

"I said it," was France's murmured retort.

The five hands fell morosely silent. This man before them had met their bluff. In fact, the bluffing was all done. He wasn't buckling under, he was gaining ground every moment he faced them. What was to be done now? Their instructions, handed to them by Drood an hour ago, had been very strong but Drood hadn't mentioned the possibility of gunplay at all.

44

Even the cocksure youth with the pale face had sobered down. That tall stranger looked pretty competent up there on the porch. By degrees they switched attention to their own spokesman. It was his decision.

The spokesman scratched his whiskers and came to a stand. "Don't you want to live?" he grunted.

"Pull the trunks down," said France softly.

"Then, damn you, take what you got comin'—"

The rest of the crew failed to follow his lead. He was the only one to go for his gun, and he never got the kink out of his elbow. France hitched himself curiously, and bent forward. The barrel of his revolver swung toward the five ranch hands like an accusing finger.

"You fellows take too much time making up your minds," observed France. "And you telegraphed your intentions five seconds ahead of the draw, Whiskers. Turn around, all of you."

They obeyed, having no more to say then. France slipped their guns with a nimble wariness and backed to the porch. "Now pull those trunks into the house."

"You had oughta got Kidder to come up here," growled the spokesman. "How in thunder did we know?"

"You've got a pretty good idea," replied France.

"I doubt you'll ever sleep in that house," prophesied the spokesman, bending his back to a trunk. "I sure doubt it, and I ain't meanin' that I'm goin' to try to put you out, either. They's others."

France took the collected artillery into the bedroom

and methodically threw bedding, clothes, and all other accumulated personal effects through the door. The spokesman protested glumly. "Say, that's my stuff."

"You're down a peg," said France. "You sleep in the bunkhouse. Looks like a hog has been wallowing around here. Set 'em down and get out. Unhitch that team. Whiskers, you get that front gate fixed before it falls apart. There's a mower sitting out in the yard about rusted to pieces. Pull it in the shed. Get busy. Any comments?"

"Not now," said Whiskers.

"Then prod along."

They dragged their spurs out of the place. France opened a trunk, pulled out a saddle and accompanying gear and tossed the captured guns in. Locking the trunk, he kicked it against the wall.

"Expect they've got more firearms around the place," he thought, "but it's my guess they won't move till they get some plainer orders. The last directions didn't work well for them. It's clear to me there's some big fellow behind this business. Question now is, who?"

The Chinaman came slipping across the room in felt slippers. "You come eat. This time allight. Nex' time you come quick allsame other boys. I no run allday restaurant."

France grinned and looked at his watch. Near two o'clock and his first day in the country half gone. "That's a good idea, Sam. But unless I'm mistaken your star boarders are going to eat irregular for a few weeks. How long you been here?"

"Fi'teen year. You come."

France went into the ell of the cabin that contained kitchen and dining room. He ate a good stout meal with a gusto that seemed to please the Oriental and then went out and sat on the porch to consider the situation over a cigarette. A man was hammering away at the front gate. The mower had been pulled into the shed. The rest of the crew were out of sight. They had apparently given in to his authority, but he was wiser than to believe this would last. They would send the news of his arrival to wherever the man higher up in this affair happened to be. Then hostilities would start again.

The more France considered it, the more he was convinced that Golloway was serving only as a cog in somebody else's wheel. Golloway was a gunman and not a leader. He took his orders and executed them, as these five hands on the ranch were doing. Drood was an unknown factor to France. But there was a curious situation here. The man himself was unfriendly while his daughter seemed distinctly on the other side of the fence. Kidder also was an enigma. France judged that the lawyer's morals were capable of infinite stretching, but he still had no proof that the putty-fleshed creature was doing anything other than winking at some third party's illegality. What then? What man held the power to set a tide of resistance against him almost instantly?

"Seems to be no bottom to the well," France thought, grinding his cigarette beneath a boot heel. "But I believe Slim Hillis will have some ideas on that. Meanwhile, shall I tell these buzzards they're fired tonight or had I better wait till morning?"

After some amount of low deliberation, France decided that he would wait until Hillis came in the morning. That was his ace in the hole—the fact that he had already found support from a man like Hillis—and he didn't want to reveal it too soon. If he fired the crew tonight they would guess he was expecting help elsewhere and that knowledge would instantly be relayed to the unknown leader in the background. Better wait, better have the advantage of one night's comparative peace.

Rising, he went inside to an old-fashioned desk— Ike France's catch-all for business papers. Rather half-heartedly he looked for an account book that would reveal the full extent of the IF range and the amount of stock grazing thereon. But, as he expected, he didn't find anything to help him. Either Kidder held all the valuable papers or else they had been stolen. Probably stolen, because otherwise Kidder would have surrendered them to him that morning. After two hour's patient digging through the papers and letters remaining, John France pushed in the drawers and pulled down the desk cover. As he did so he at last knew what his job was to be.

I've inherited an outfit," he told himself, "but that's only a small item. I've inherited a quarrel which I've got to take up and carry through. I have got to hunt around for cattle probably drifted all over hell's half acre. I have got to run down—unless all first hand evidence is wrong—enough rustled stuff to stock an ordinary outfit. I've got to find out who's behind all this mess and stop him dead. And that's not all of the story either. I've got to uncover a little something about Ike's sudden death, which doesn't sound satisfactory the way Kidder tells it. On top of that there's the main proposition of my being able to survive a lot of immediate punishment. Happy days."

He went to the bedroom and got his saddle gear. Going from the house he met Whiskers coming in. The spokesman of the group had completely changed his attitude, and was as near to friendliness as he would ever get.

"Anything more you want done?" he asked France, falling in step as the latter aimed for the corral.

"Too late to do anything today," said France. "I want a horse."

"We drove in the saddle bunch from the hills yesterday," said Whiskers and pointed through the bars. "That bay yonder I been usin' in my string. He's one fine horse. Take him."

"I'll give it a try," agreed France, walking into the corral. Whiskers watched him closely as he shook out his twine, built a loop and snapped it over the milling horses. The bay hauled around and came to a docile stand.

"You understand," said Whiskers. "We boys had to

49

be plumb careful. Lots of crooked stuff bein' pulled around here. Don't take it unfriendly we was dubious about you. All for the good of the ranch."

"Handsome sentiments," was France's laconic answer. He slapped the saddle on the bay and cinched up. Over his shoulder he threw a casual question. "How much stuff have I got out on the range?"

"Shucks, I dunno," was Whiskers prompt answer. "The ranch bein' sort of tied up thisaway, we didn't hold no beef roundup last fall—and ain't had no orders so far to make a spring tally. So I sure couldn't say."

"Can't even make a guess, huh?" asked France, coaxing the bay to quit swelling against the latigo.

"I'd be wrong if I tried. Kidder had ought to know."

France stepped up to the saddle and walked the horse out of the corral, Whiskers coming behind to close the gate.

"This is a blamed fine pony," stated France. "So Kidder has been giving all the orders since Ike died?"

"Yeah," said Whiskers, after a cautious interval of thought. "Uh-huh. Why?"

"Just wondered. How big a range have I got? Where's the corners?"

Whiskers was still vague. "I'd have to ride around to show you. Can't see far in this rough country."

"Where's the stuff grazing now?"

"Well, they's a bunch yonder." He pointed westward. "And some higher in the hills and some down below. Got some over east likewise. Ain't rode out

50

much so far this year. Can't say just where they done drifted. Kidder never give us no orders to ride close."

"Where's my neighbors?"

On this point Whiskers grew more definite. "Six miles over the hump to west is Laurel Annison. North from her and us about eight miles is Al McQuarter. Four miles east of McQuarter's is Drood's. Still more east Golloway has got a small outfit, half critters and half horses."

"Not a crowded country," reflected France, scratching the bay behind an ear. "This is a blamed fine animal. And what's north of those outfits?"

Whiskers was studying France quite closely as if trying to make out the meaning of all this questioning. "Why, nothin' much. The pass runs up six thousand feet and goes across to a country I don't know personal. About forty miles yonder is a railroad construction outfit. I guess—"

A rider appeared between the pines of the western slope, zigzagging down the steep trail. Whiskers stopped talking and moved forward a little to study this visitor. Presently the rider threw himself across the creek and cantered along the yard, sweeping it with a restless glance. France chuckled softly as he made out the freckle-faced Annison puncher who had delivered a message from Laurel Annison that morning. It appeared this was another such errand, and the rider's chubby pigmented face seemed a little surly as he drew rein and passed a slip of paper across to France.

"This is your busy day delivering things, ain't it?" grinned France.

"I've done more important chores," the rider said, and never so much as ducked his head at Whiskers. "Usual, I don't stray into this territory."

"It's a wise man that knows his proper business," said Whiskers with an irritating turn to the words.

"Too damn bad everybody ain't that wise then," replied the freckle-faced rider.

France opened the note to discover Laurel Annison's forthright personality contained in it:

You're a darn big fool, John France. Better men than you have bucked this country and lost. In case you have no previous engagements drop over. There's an extra plate on the table tonight.

Laurel Annison

The swift downstroke of her writing matched the picture she had made in town that morning—sure and self-confident. France tucked the note in his pocket. "Tell her I'll do just that, with many thanks."

"Didn't think you'd dast turn her down twice runnin'," said the freckled one and whirled away.

Whiskers spat on the ground. "Stiff-necked outfit. They think they're awful damn good. Say, that's a slick saddle you got."

France nodded and watched the disappearing rider. He rode the bay around the yard and came up to the house again. "You tell Sam I won't be home for supper," he said to Whiskers. "May be pretty late when I get back."

"Be goin' to Annisons?" asked Whiskers, the smoky eyes fastening on France's face.

France nodded and rode across the creek. Up among the pines he turned to look down at the ranch quarters. All five of the hands were clustered together in the yard, talking earnestly. He shook his head and followed the trail around a bulging shoulder of rock.

"Awfully friendly for a change," he mused. "But that's only a disguise. They've got something up their sleeves. Expect they'll find those guns, but it doesn't matter much."

The trail kept him climbing along the slope of the rising ridge for half an hour then took him through a mountain meadow, green and glistening under the late sunlight. Even as he crossed it the sun sank below the cones and spires of the vast range and the cobalt shadows came swirling down. The meadows puckered in to another small pass and France found himself riding halfway between heaven and earth with a cliff to one side and a view of remote little valleys far below on the other. The air sharpened. Coyotes yammered somewhere above. A jet of water cascaded through a fissure of the cliff side and rumbled beneath a plank bridge.

Then in the isolation and the peace of a mountain evening he arrived before the mouth of a draw that ran higher into the rugged country. Roads forked and a mailbox as big as a dog house sat in the shadows with the Annison name and brand—Window Pane.

France turned into the draw, ascended the curving road and at last embarked on another meadow ringed around by hills. There was activity here, the movement of a ranch alive with business. A yellow light gushed from the door of the main house. When he rode to the porch he saw Laurel Annison's piquant face looking up at him from a rocking chair. Beside her was the smiling, quizzical countenance of a wiry man of his own age. The man's hat was off and a shock of sandy hair fell down to form a cowlick across a pleasant forehead.

They both rose. Laurel Annison came forward to the steps and held out a hand as France stepped down. She gave his answering palm a firm, quick pressure and spoke with a cool casualness. "So you decided to be friendly for a change, Mr. France? I'm really glad to meet you, though after throwing myself at you and being rejected I probably ought to be good and mad."

France chuckled. "I got your note and came on the run. I've been told it wasn't wise to keep you waiting."

The man on the porch grinned broadly, whereat Laurel Annison said, "Let me introduce you gentlemen. John France, this is Al McQuarter who runs the Diamond and a Half north of you. Al, this is the man who snubbed me in Crowheart."

"Now I wouldn't say that," France said as McQuarter shook hands with a quick and hearty manner. "I told your rider to tell you I had a little business on my chest and would be right along."

"We have heard about that business already," said Laurel Annison. "You work fast, don't you?"

"Better say the other side works fast," drawled France.

"So you've discovered there is another side?" inquired the girl, throwing a significant glance toward McQuarter.

McQuarter spoke for the first time, changing the subject. "Laurel, your taste seems to run to towheads. I thought I had yellow hair but France has got me cheated."

The girl looked up to France and then with a sudden imperious gesture shoved him into the path of light to observe him better. "My land, Al, he's tall. That isn't yellow, it's corn-tassel gold. I don't see why the Lord gave you hair, Mr. France, that a girl would be pleased to have. Al, they said he was a pilgrim, but I'll bet a hat he's from Texas."

McQuarter chuckled, an infectious good humor bubbling up. "Don't mind Laurel, France. She never did understand why it ain't fashionable to ask direct questions. Women are thataway."

"I didn't ask one," protested Laurel, shaking her head. "I only hinted."

"Wrong guess," murmured France. "I was practically born in the Comstock Lode. I'm a Nevadan."

"Well, it's time to eat," said the girl. "Come in."

She started to lead the way and stopped, hearing the drum of a rapidly approaching horseman. A soft and urgent, "Al," floated over the yard. McQuarter turned quickly and walked from the porch and stood talking with the messenger. Presently he came back, apologetic. "Say, I'm blamed sorry about this. I've got to hustle back to the ranch." The wiry frame of the man straightened and his cheerful face soberly inclined towards France. "I'm glad you moved into this country. It can stand more good men and I hated to see the Circle IF go idle so long. I want you to know that if there's ever anything in the line of help you want, call on me. I mean that. Seein' as how we're the only two good lookin' yellow-haired gents around Crowheart we ought to stick together."

"Thanks," drawled France and held his peace. He was trying to make out the face of the distant rider but could see nothing but a blurred form.

"Darn!" exclaimed Laurel Annison. "Here I go and cook a good supper for the man on the very night I practically promised to marry him and he runs out on me. You two boys have given me a bad day."

McQuarter was already on his way to his horse, but the ripple of his laugh came back. "I'm leavin' a blamed good substitute, Laurel."

France grinned. "That's a bet. I'll try to fill in."

Laurel Annison put her arm through his elbow and looked up to him with a speculative, half-lidded glance. Then she smiled and color came to her cheeks. "You sound," she murmured, "quite capable of doing a good job of it." And lifting her words out to the yard, she added, "All right, Al. But you may be sorry for trusting a substitute. Mr. France, come along. The head of the table is for you. I hope you can carve better than Al. With all his virtues he's rotten at it."

## CHAPTER IV

Some six or seven miles deeper and higher in the rugged hills stood the sprawling quarters of Drood's Box D. In every sense it was an isolated, secretive location, for although the pass connecting the Crowheart country with the level plains northward crossed the range within half a mile of the outfit and a dozen small trails led out from Drood's front door, the contour of the land hemmed the outfit in, preventing surprise or observation. From the adjacent ridge Drood's lookout commanded every approach and every advancing traveler. At the same time the pin-grouped draws and ravines made perfect avenues of departures, arrival or concealment for members of the ranch. And this night, within the rambling living room of the house three men gathered in front of the fireplace and took the riding chill from their bones.

"Deuce Evernight is waitin' in the bunkhouse now for our orders on the subject," Drood said. "That France ain't easy discouraged. The minute he piled off the train at Crowheart, Kidder notified Sheriff Poco Finn what he came for. Poco rode out to where I was loadin' beef. I come to town, sighted the situation and told Dan to saunter over to Ziegler's and sort of discourage the pilgrim. Nothin' like startin' out soon. We got no business lettin' him reach first base. So Dan did—"

Golloway broke in and spoke for himself. "The scantlin' son of a buzzard took me off guard. How'd I know he carried a gun in his coat? He sloughed me down, busted a front grinder and snapped a piece on me! I ain't through with him by a long drink and a run!"

"Well," proceeded Drood, "he started for the ranch. I cut around and got to Circle IF ahead of him, and I give Deuce Evernight strict orders he wasn't to let France stable his horses. Told Deuce to stall France off, make the gent go back and get Kidder's written orders. By which delay I meant we should have some time to get organized on the subject and cover up our tracks. They're too damn plain as things are now. But I got to hand it to France. He cowed Evernight and the other four boys and moved in. Evernight said he'd of shot the buckles off France's coat the minute said gent rode through the gate if he'd had orders thataway. But he was dubious what to do and let France get the bulge. France took the boys' guns away from them. Can you digest that?"

The third man, listening to all this with an ill-concealed impatience was Al McQuarter, just ridden in from Laurel Annison's. He was no longer smiling and no longer pleasant. Anger shimmered in his gray eyes. Long, transverse lines sprang across the wiry face.

"We got to do somethin'," said Drood more strongly. "He's caught us with our shirts half off. Once he starts pokin' around for his critters he's goin' to find enough to send all of us on a vacation."

"So you tried the old gag of tenderfootin' him?" challenged McQuarter. "Couldn't you see with one eye he wasn't that kind of a fellow? That man is a fighter from away back. He knows this game and all its dodges just as well as you or I. I knew it the minute I saw him—and I didn't get more than one look in the dark at that."

"How'd we know?" grumbled Big Dan Golloway. "He comes to town like any other tourist, wearin' dude clothes and talkin' smooth like a dude. How'd we know?"

"Neither one of you has got sense enough to fill a gander's head," retorted McQuarter. "All you've succeeded in doing is to open his eyes and make him cagey."

"He don't know where I stand," put in Drood. "I'm still under cover."

"I ain't!" was Golloway's bitter remark. "Damn, I'm always the guy that has to be the target. I'm tired of it."

Drood's swart, beetling cheeks veered toward McQuarter. "Listen," said he, cold and grim, "I don't like your remarks about my intelligence. What would you do if you got such a master mind?"

"I would have let him take his ranch without a protest. I'd be perfectly friendly with him. In fact, tonight I told him if he wanted any help to be sure and call on me."

"Yeah," growled Golloway, "you would put yourself under cover."

"Because I know a better way," replied McQuarter sharply. "Let him have his ranch. He doesn't know the country. He's got to have help to run it. He'll have to use the five men already on it—and they're doing just what we tell them to do."

"Supposin' he fired 'em right off the bat?" demanded Drood.

"Then," replied McQuarter, "he'll have to hire others. And we'll see he hires the kind of men we want him to have. I tell you, he doesn't know anybody in this country. He's got to go it blind and take what he gets. Let him have the ranch. We'll be the same as running it, getting our own affairs in order. When we're through he won't have enough meat for breakfast. The key to the situation is to keep feeding men who'll do what we tell them to do."

It ain't so easy as it sounds," disagreed Drood. "Not by a jugful. Once he gets holt of the records of the ranch he'll know he's been rustled poor, and he'll be on the prod."

McQuarter was openly contemptuous. "Use your head! I've already had Kidder burn every scrap of records he could find on the place. Of course, he can guess. And since he's a pretty shrewd party he will do a lot of guessin'. But by the time he gets squared around we'll have him cleaned out. There is one thing we've got to do right away."

"Yeah?"

McQuarter paused. Louise Drood came from the kitchen and idled around some magazines on the table, seeming uninterested in their talk. McQuarter's gray eyes rested on her, enigmatic, half-closed. The girl felt the force of his inspection and looked up, vivid face flushing a little.

"Haven't seen much of you lately, Al," said she. "The other flame burns brighter these days, doesn't it?"

"Cut it out, Louise," drawled McQuarter. Something passed between them. Her shoulders rose slightly, and she turned away to hide the sudden fire of her eyes.

"Not that it makes any difference to me," she added.

"Now, now." McQuarter grinned. "Don't you love me any more, Louise? Not throwing me over?"

"Better be careful, Al. A woman has some out-landish weapons."

McQuarter sobered and checked his talk. Drood grunted at his daughter. "Get out of here, Louise. We got business."

She swung on them. "Don't you suppose I know what it's all about? I'm not deaf, dumb and blind. Don't be so foolish." She started up the stairs but stopped on the landing to call back. "I'm going to town in the morning and buy a lot of clothes, Pop."

When she was gone McQuarter chuckled.

"That's what I call blackmail, Drood."

Drood shrugged his shoulders. "That girl ought to

have a mother. She's past me any more."

"Has been for some time," observed McQuarter and rolled a cigarette. Drood's face darkened and he stared at McQuarter a long while. Whatever was on his tongue, he dismissed it and changed the subject.

"We got to stop France. That's all."

"There's one thing we've got to do right away," continued McQuarter. "And that's to run off that Circle IF bunch we've been nursing toward the end of the Cottonwood Meadow. Quicker the better. You tell Evernight to hustle home and drag his men up to the meadow. You take a few of your own hands and send them on to help. Run the stuff up beyond, through the same place we used last time."

"So I should do it and get myself in trouble?" queried Drood. "You're awful careful to keep your own skirts clean, ain't you?"

"Which I been sayin' all the time," added Golloway morosely.

McQuarter could turn as hard as stone with one shift of his cheeks. He did so now. "We've talked that all over. I take care of my end, don't I? What more do you want? I never thought you two fellows would turn yellow because of one man. Cut it out. We're as safe as a bank if we hop to and clean up our affairs in a hurry. So get busy on that Cottonwood Meadow right away tonight."

"I suppose you'll got back to lop around Laurel Annison while we're doin' it,' jeered Golloway.

McQuarter's whole face blackened. "Damn you,

Golloway, keep your tongue off that girl or I'll kill you!"

"Now stop that, both of you!" Drood said. It's poor business for partners to disagree over women. It's his business, Dan. But I tell you both right now my idea of the whole mess. We have got to kill him off. One France went that way, why not another?"

"Always heavy-handed, Drood," objected McQuarter. "There is a time for that, but not until other ways fail."

"So?" broke in Golloway. "Well that's my style just like it's Drood's. He belted me down and made a sucker out of me to Crowheart. I got a notion to lay over the town trail and pop him from the rocks. It's the easiest way."

The three of them fell solemnly silent. McQuarter smoked on his cigarette, studying the fire with veiled eyes. Drood averted his face from Golloway who had stiffened into a sullen rage and stared boldly at them both.

Presently McQuarter's weighing glance passed over Golloway and he said softly, "Well, its up to you, Dan. Maybe it is the best way. If you pull it we're certainly shut of the France tribe. I'll say neither yes nor no. It is strictly your private affair and I never want to hear anything more about it. Now, having missed a fine supper I'll canter home to a cold snack."

He passed through the back way and to his horse tethered in the darkness. Riding home he weighed all possibilities in his shrewd unsentimental mind. He hadn't changed his mind about using gunplay on France because he believed it to be the easiest way. He disliked violence when it was unnecessary. But Golloway was the weak link in the partnership and gradually losing usefulness. If the gunman succeeded in his purpose, then France was out of the road. But if Golloway's first shot went wide he was the same as dead. Al McQuarter was too shrewd a judge of men not to recognize the caliber of John France. The slim and casual newcomer, if he survived the first shot, would be more than a match for the gunman. He would kill Golloway. And that was all right. It would serve McQuarter's purpose quite well.

. So he rode home to get his snack and, what was more important, to establish an alibi against tonight's rustling party. Outside of his partners and a few punchers and Louise Drood, nobody else knew that it was he who had created the vast and lawless ring that controlled the country. He guided and ruled it. He directed its every move and all others were his tools.

After he left the house Golloway also pulled out, and Drood went to the crew's quarters to give Evernight the necessary orders. Louise Drood, hidden on the second story landing, rose from her cramped covert. She was trembling and her small fists were gripped painfully tight. She had overheard all this, as she had overheard a great many other such conferences. In the past none of this outlawry ever bothered her for the Drood morals were all she had ever known. But tonight she crept to her room and went to a sleepless bed, thinking of the slim, yellow-haired France.

"No more pie? No more coffee?"

"If I took another morsel I'd bust," decided John France. "You must be trying to plump me up for market."

"Then let's move over by the fire,' said Laurel. "I doubt if anything could ever put fat on you, Mr. France. You're just naturally one of the long, slow, slim-hipped clan. My dad was like you up to the last day of his life."

They sat beside the fire, face to face over the stone hearth, while a motherly housekeeper cleared the table and left them alone. The girl suddenly rose and took a cigar from the mantel and passed it to France. "That was meant for Al," she explained, bending down to light a slip of paper. And as she held it before the cigar she added, "But I hope you enjoy it more than he would have."

He looked at her through the trailing smoke, the gray eyes quite sober. "It's been many years since anything like this has happened to me."

"Thank you. That is a very nice compliment."

All during the meal John France had been revising his conception of this strange girl. The picture he had of her riding through Crowheart revealed only a small part of her real nature. Tonight the riding clothes were gone, the brisk self-confidence gone. She sat before him with her white hands lying sedately in her lap, her head falling against the chair's back in pure relaxation. Against the sheer, low-cut edge of her dress her white throat held a pearl color and her features were softly beautiful in the lamp's glow. He was aware again of the piquancy of her face and its sudden moments of expressiveness, and his glance kept drifting to the heavy lustrousness of her auburn hair.

She was of course aware of the rather penetrating inspection. In another man it would have irritated her, would have seemed boorish. But she had recognized in John France at the first meeting a strong sense of reserve and self-control; the qualities of a gentleman. There was nothing overbearing in his gaze. Rather it was the grave and full appraisal of a man who wanted to confirm his own beliefs. So she kept the lazy silence, in turn marking the strong, bronzed outline of his head. Nature had cut and kept his features in a bold line from nose to chin and then, as if to draw the pattern to a fine balance, had tapered him magnificently from the broad shoulders and flat chest down to the narrowing hips. In the chair he seemed lazy and tired and easy-going; but as she caught an unexpected depth of light in the steady gray eyes she had the sure conviction that he held within him a dynamic latent power. There was, as well, something suggesting unusual strength in the long, tanned fingers with the cords showing above the skin even in rest.

He moved the cigar idly in front of him. "This is no way for me to act, like an old granny wearing slippers. I'd better perk up."

"Just you enjoy that smoke and let me do the talking. I've been wondering if you expected the sort of a situation you've come into."

"In a way. No man's got a right to expect the impossible. Here's a well-stocked ranch lying ownerless for half a year. I've never seen a cattle country yet without rustling and this section is no exception. I figured that much from the beginning. But I'll admit I wasn't quite prepared to have 'em jump me before I had a chance to change clothes."

"You mean about Golloway?"

"Uh-huh."

"Did you have any trouble at the ranch?"

"A slight argument."

She leaned forward. "I thought that might happen. Oh, it's such a darn shame. That's what made me write that fool note. I'm sorry. But do you know what I intended to say to you tonight? I was going to offer to buy your ranch. I could use that range very well and it meant an easy way out for you."

"Changed your mind?" he drawled.

"You're not the kind to sell," she said.

"Thanks. It's about right."

"But you can't go along with that crew, Mr. France. I refuse to tell tales but I do know you'll never get along with them. I was wondering if you'd let me lend you a part of my crew while you got acquainted with the country."

He debated telling her of his plans and finally decided to. "Between you and me, Miss Annison, I've made a little gamble on human nature already. I took a chance on a man's face and gave him the job of

67

finding me a half-dozen fighters."

She shot, "Who?" at him so energetically that he smiled.

"Slim Hillis."

"Oh, Slim. I don't know whether you are lucky or have the wisdom of a serpent. If you can run Slim he will run your ranch. There's always been a place open on my outfit for him but he wouldn't work for a woman. He's a hard little fighter himself. Even so, you're not out of the woods. I won't say anything against any man and I won't name any names, but they have a stranglehold on your ranch, Mr. France. For that matter the whole country is gripped by the same gang. I've been very lucky. Haven't lost a single head of beef or even found a rustler's trail on my range. Somebody's very chivalrous, I suppose. Or again it may be the fact that I carry a big outfit and also that—" she paused and looked straight into his eyes—"that I have as a good friend a gentleman who, though he isn't a gunman, has the record of being the quickest and best shot in this territory. A rustler is a coward, and there isn't a one who'd dare touch Al McQuarter."

"I sort of guessed he was sudden with his artillery," murmured France and turned his eyes to the fire.

Laurel Annison watched him, a small frown puckering her fine forehead. "When he said you were to call on him for any help, he meant that. You can trust his word all the way."

France nodded and a long quiet fell over the room. Laurel Annison's cheeks bloomed to a slow rose color

68

and one small high-heeled slipper took to tapping the floor. When she spoke again she too was looking into the fire. "I like folks to know about me, Mr. France. I always like to keep the record straight. Perhaps I gave you the wrong impression about myself and Al McQuarter. He and I—well, there has been a long, long question between us. It isn't—quite so settled as I seemed to indicate when I told you we were practically engaged. We both grew up in this country. After all 'practically' is a very indefinite word, isn't it?"

France had finished the cigar. He threw it in the fire and turned to her. "Miss Annison, you do know how to give a man a perfect evening. After what you've said I'm going home and roll rocks down the mountain just because I feel good."

The color on her cheeks grew deeper. Then, after a self-conscious interval, their glances crossed and of a sudden they were both laughing. France rose reluctantly. "McQuarter made a misplay when he used me as a substitute." Then he grew grave. "I don't mean it so lightly either when I say that I'm a sort of overweening cuss and I might try to step up a notch from this substitute business."

She turned the subject. "You haven't asked me any questions about the country. I'd be glad to tell you all I can."

"The things I want to know at present," he answered, "are not what you'd care to tell me. It's my own battle. Do you understand what I mean?"

She nodded, taking a deep, swift breath and

speaking hurriedly. "Yes, but please remember the men against you will stop at nothing at all. I don't wish to meddle in your affairs. Only—well, take an old-timer's words and watch your back-trail every minute."

The slow smile returned to his lean cheeks. "I have never spent a more pleasant evening, Miss Annison. And the funny thing is I came over here expecting to quarrel with you."

"But you don't know me very well. You haven't seen the bad side of me."

"I'd take the chance to find out."

She tilted her chin and veered to mock seriousness. "Mr. France, do you mean that or are you just trying to tamper with an innocent girl's affections?"

"I mean it."

"Then I shall see that you get the chance."

So they stood a moment longer, the tall and yellow-haired man tipping his head toward this girl with the fair, expressive face. Once again there was the steady appraisal, the long meeting of eyes. Then John France bowed and passed into the darkness.

At the throat of the meadow he swung to see her outlined in the ranchhouse door and with that picture he cantered down the trail to the mailbox and turned east on the main road, a far different man from the John France who a few hours earlier had ridden up to the Annison yard. He traveled with the blood stirring fresh and strong in his veins and a high hope singing through head and heart. The weariness and the worry of the long day dropped from his shoulders, the problem in front of him was for the time dissolved by the magic of a woman's clear and splendid face and the slow, throaty melody of her words. For him this evening represented the great turning point of all his twenty-four years. After many thousand miles the narrow and turbulent trail of his life suddenly came out upon a fair land.

"I think, pony," he drawled, "that I've got a chance. This McQuarter fellow has the inside track on me. Tonight I was nothing but second best, eating another man's meal and smoking another man's cigar. I don't know why I ought to be hopeful about it, but I've been fighting most of my life for the things I have wanted and, by Jupiter, I'll fight for this!"

He curled around the lip of the abyss, pursued the winding road along the grade and arrived at the mountain meadow. Properly, he ought to have gone home, but the night held a full, rare savor and he felt the need of riding off the heady exultation of spirit gripping him. So he turned left from the trail and struck deeper into the meadow.

It was very dark, with the clouds of spring blotting out stars and moon and the land to either side no more than distorted shadows of rock and slope and tree merging into a shapeless mass. The heavy air misted against his cheeks, the hoofs of his horse slid sibilantly through the damp grass. Along this sharp and thin fog a muffled coyote's chant was carried to mingle with the subdued tinkle of his bridle chains and the slight squeaking of saddle leather. And down from the pines rolled the steady abrasion of a slow wind to slide into the upward rustle of the small creatures of the earth. The mystery of the night was full upon him.

He had no exact knowledge of where he quested. Earlier in the evening when he had crossed the meadow westbound he had observed that it ran away a considerable distance to the northward, canalling into the surrounding ridges as it went. He had also observed the marks of cattle and it was his belief that he was now on his own range. Probably his own cattle were grazing yonder; or if not his, then Annison's. Thinking thus he was arrested by quick, dim detonations of sound to the front—the moving of hurrying hoofs. He was at that moment in the process of rolling a cigarette but the tobacco spilled to the ground as he halted his horse and listened more closely. There could be no doubt. That drumming, rising to sudden spurts, dying, and rising again, could be made only by ridden horses.

He forced his pony on at a quiet pace, all his faculties pinching down to one channel of hard reasoning. He was too old at the game not to understand this. Men didn't cut in and out like that unless they were bunching critters, and no lawful outfit worked under the cloak of darkness. The sounds grew louder. Someone charged directly toward him and circled with a squeaking of gear. A muffled voice came along, "All right—drag up! We're on our way." Another instant and John France was beside the cattle and beside more men. They were pressing against the herd, moving it out of a walk to a shuffling trot; a rider swung close enough to brush one of his stirrups and an impatient mutter reached him. "Let's go, then! Don't dally—get in and boost 'em!"

Cattle and rustlers galloped along the meadow, momentum carrying all into the deeper, more towering shadows. France touched the butt of his gun and rode with them.

## CHAPTER V

A voice, vaguely familiar to France, sounded from the right front. "Pinch 'em in more or we'll be scattered all over the damn country!" The riders near France quartered away, the speed slackened, the walls of the ridge suddenly closed in. They were filing steeply up, the line of cattle lengthening and the sound of the point rustlers growing fainter. For a while France was alone and in this period his mind raced down the alleys of action open to him. His impulse to play a hand in this dangerous game had been actuated by a belief that he might uncover the leading spirits of the ring that seemed to control the Crowheart country. The kingpins of the ring would probably not be in this foray but out of the confusion and in the swift phrases shuttering back and forth he hoped to hear names mentioned that would be of use to him.

France wanted also to discover where the rustlers were taking the cattle. And that brought him face to face with the need for a quick decision. Once he discovered the rendezvous, should he break away or should he wait for daylight to reveal the party? Within a mile of steady advance, in which he was sometimes alone, sometimes flanked by hard-breathing men, he decided he had better get clear once they rounded the herd and held it. If they discovered his presence they would intensify their efforts to destroy him. Otherwise, they might leave him alone long enough for him to put his knowledge to account.

The pace had further diminished and he was aware that one of the party stuck persistently to the herd's rear and also very near by. There was a danger in this continued proximity and France turned and flanked the cattle. This brought him up along the side of a ridge and close to another of the riders. Gradually he dropped away and established a solitary position. The runway between the ridges shot to a difficult angle and slackened to an area of smooth bench. They were rather high, and a wind freshened against them and the night fog was thinner. A quarter-hour later cattle and men were dipping along another face of the rugged country, turning as well to a different direction of the compass. The readjustment brought France again to the rear and he felt the presence of a man plodding beside him—the same one he had previously left.

The constant variation of course and the opaque sky blurred his sense of place and the uneven gait blurred the measuring of time. Downgrade the rustlers broke the bunch into a stiff-footed gallop. Upgrade they crawled. But for an hour, or it might have been twice that time, the dipping and rising was only a part of an insistent march toward some high point in the range. Presently they reached it, the shadows paling around them and the land below seeming like a rolling, lightless ocean.

There was a brief halt. The man beside France rode ahead, leaving him alone. And in this intermission France drew clear. Then they were traveling onward in a straighter, surer line. Another hour went by and at the end of it they plunged head first down a chutelike cut in the earth and were absorbed by shadows thick enough to slice.

Far below them a single ray of light shimmered through the fog, then vanished and was not seen again until they cleared an area of trees. But for two miles or better this beacon continued to wink and vanish. A murmur ran back. The man beside France said, "Lean away and see that left flank don't straggle into Glide's Gulch."

France checked and turned. Another rustler crossed in front of him, swearing softly.

All of a sudden the light was on top of them, swinging forward in a man's fist, and they were in a mushbowl depression. It happened so swiftly that the cattle were milling before France had time to pull himself out of the situation. And while he sat like a statue in the saddle, all faculties strained, he heard a cautious shifting of riders about him, a murmured challenge from the lantern bearer and some swift half-whispered reply.

"What next?" queried the same tantalizingly familiar voice.

"You boys can drift home," replied the man with the lantern. The light shifted and rose, to give France a view of Big Dan Golloway's angular and sullen face. "This stuff lays over here till day after tomorrow and then takes the other trip. We'll take care of it."

"Then what the hell is the hurry in the first place?" growled the unknown party.

"Orders," the gunman said. "Ain't you learned better than to question orders from the chief? The big idea is, we wanted to snake this Circle IF stuff out of Cottonwood before that yella-haired France mug got to pokin' around. In the next couple of weeks we got to rustle that—" and Golloway's lurid, bitter epithets snapped hot and venomous through the mist—"clean down to his spare britches."

"If he finds out we're in this deal," said the invisible speaker, "he'll sure make a play at us."

At that instant France knew this man. It was Whiskers, the foreman who had contested his right to take over the ranch. Meanwhile Golloway was talking on. "Well, you got five guns, ain't you?"

A rider beside France closed in slowly until his stirrup touched that of the Circle IF's new owner. "Got a match?"

France's arm dropped toward his gun, but he managed a muffled, grunted "No," and waited. Nothing happened. Whiskers embarked on an angry speech.

"Yeah, we got five guns. Took 'em out of this alleged dude's trunks where he'd hid 'em. And nobody can tell me he's a dude after the way he manipulated that draw on we boys. But supposin' we have got guns? We're supposed to be workin' under orders, and I ain't heard no plain, downright, unvarnished words so far that calls for shootin' it out. What's the matter with you big bugs? Can't you make up your minds what to do? We'd of nailed him at the front gate this noon if Drood had of only talked turkey. Instead he beats around the bush and says we ain't to let France pile his blankets on the bed. What's that mean? It could mean anything, but it don't sound like a shootin' scrape. I want somethin' definite on the subject."

"Well," said Golloway, "you know me, boys. I'm for direct action all the time. So's Drood now. But this mornin' he didn't know the caliber of this France jasper. Him and me is agreed at present. Howsomever, you well know we ain't runnin' the party. I think—"

"Wait a minute," said a rider adjoining France. "How many in this bunch right now?"

"What you mean?"

"Somethin' fishy runnin' along my wishbone. Five from Circle IF. Four Drood boys, ain't it—and Dan there? That's ten. Well, I'll just bet my watch and chain against a double-hole doughnut they's more than ten sittin' in the leather this minute."

Golloway flung the lantern high over his head and

bore it nearer the group in great strides. At the same moment the rustler nearest France crowded full against him and challenged, "Did you say you had a match? Sing out so's I can hear your voice?" The extreme edge of the light touched the muzzle of France's horse and Whiskers—Deuce Evernight by his real name—yelled a warning. But the light got no closer. France had drawn and placed a shot into the veering globe. The flame leaped and died. Golloway cried a mighty order and, in defiance to every rule of safety, he threw a bullet at the spot where he had seen France's weapon spit fire.

But France had moved. At the same time he had put his gun to use he had swung his pony sharp around and beat past two or three rustlers blocking the way. Deuce Evernight was shouting at Golloway to put up his gun. Golloway hurled a string of roaring oaths toward the party and threatened to fire again. "I hear that sonofabuck! He's tryin' to break clear! Ram him—ram him! Somebody knock him outen the saddle afore he busts loose!"

A hand swept out and struck France in the face. His horse ploughed into another rustler broadside and the impact sent the fellow to the ground. But there was an arm clutching at his coat and a yell of discovery ringing in his ear. Swinging as far as he dared from the saddle, he sliced the barrel of his gun outward and across the cramped darkness. A man bawled in agony and the detaining fist fell away. The road seemed clear. He set his spurs and forged ahead. Immediately the guns began speaking at him and the slugs ripped up the earth before and beside. He bent around, sent three quick shots at the dancing gun jets and then threw himself forward on the pony's neck. A man was panting out a broken, guttural prayer for help. "Boys—he got me! Here, I'm done for. Light a match and see can't you stop this damn blood!"

Golloway's lust for the kill came spewing out. "He's hit back to the trail! Never mind lightin' up! Go get him! Come on—I'll kill the eavesdroppin', yella-livered spawn of hell!"

France was throwing his horse loose-reined up the hill. The echo of Golloway's brutal tirade lost force through the intervening fog. The rustlers were all tangled up in the darkness, colliding with each other and held momentarily back by the pleas of the dying man. A fierce argument rose and was damped in France's ears by the pound of his mount's driving feet. That delay and argument saved him. Climbing with every ounce of strength, France's horse put the last sound of the rustlers behind, turned a shoulder of the rugged ridge and pressed on.

For a quarter-hour he gave the horse a free head. If the rustlers were pursuing he never heard them, and presently, to better verify his judgment, he stopped to rest the hard-breathing animal and to listen into the clinging fog that was thickening to a misting rain. His clothes were damp with it. His hat was gone, and a trickle of moisture fell down from his hair. The gun was still in his fist and, returning it to the holster, he *was aware* of a cramping pain along one shoulder. Somehow in the drive to get clear he had been soundly struck. Thus he paused while the fighting tension eased away and his senses sharpened to catch every stray sound in the blackness. No mutter of pursuit rose out of the depths.

"It's nine to one," he mused, "they've decided it was me that busted into their party. Isn't likely anybody else would try to horn into it. Now, that being the case I'd better bust for home. They don't appear to be following, and that isn't reasonable on their part at all. They've got another scheme up their sleeves. Pony, we've got to reach Circle IF before they beat us to it and set fire to the shebang. Now, which way is home?"

He was entirely lost. This was not a level country in which the four ends of the earth lay open to the eye. The trail of the rustlers coming from Cottonwood Meadow had twisted, dipped and risen until absolutely every vestige of direction was erased in his mind. He stood at present in a depression of a ridge and he knew that for a few yards it would lead him a true course. But once the depression petered out he would be without any sort of guide or landmark. There was, however, the horse under him and he lectured it softly.

"You're old enough to know this country. And probably Whiskers has ridden you through every foot of it, fogging my cattle. So it's up to you. Let's go home."

Still slack-reined, the horse moved upgrade and

achieved a rounding knob. France had an anxious moment as the animal slacked off and seemed to wait a signal from the rider. Since none came, he took a few tentative steps to the left and then straightened out and plodded sure-footed through the gloom. It was a gait John France never disturbed. The night wore away tediously and the damp air cut through his clothes and thoroughly chilled him. He wanted to smoke but decided against striking a light even though complete solitude seemed to ring around him.

There was not a single sign of anyone else on the trail, and even the chant and murmur of the night creatures had fallen off, by which he knew that the morning hours were running well along. Outlines of ridge and tree and knob and bluff swung by. The deep black wells of sudden canyons stood here and there while at odd intervals the pony struck straight into what seemed an impenetrable barrier. All along through the night the jaded animal traveled slowly and surely with the silent, weary rider wrapped in somber thoughts. And at last in the paling shadows, with the mists lifting from the eastern rim to admit the first violet crack of day, John France halted between the pines and looked down on the dimly visible buildings of Circle IF.

He halted, and while throwing fresh cartridges into the gun, he swept the yard from end to end. No light burned, nothing moved save a few horses in the corral. Reviewing the night's events he understood that the war was on in grim earnest and that he might easily be walking into a trap set by Whiskers and the other hands.

After being exposed, neither the crew nor Golloway would stop short of wiping out the man who had tipped over their plans. On the other hand, it was also possible that they would draw back and wait another time and other orders from the man whom Golloway had briefly mentioned as being the chief. It was within reason that Whiskers and his outfit would never return to Circle IF as caretakers.

Slipping the gun into its seat France jogged the horse slowly down the slope. "Never find out anything standing back and wondering," he decided. "I started my ownership with the policy of wading right into deep water and I think I'd better keep it up until something busts. Once I hang fire I'm gone."

He put the horse across the creek, water washing sibilantly to his passage. Just beyond he got stiffly to the ground and walked forward to the bunkhouse. The door was open. Approaching it from a safe angle he bent forward and listened for the sound of breathing and heard none. Against the dim, rising light the interior of the bunkhouse was pitch black, a pool of mystery. After a couple of minutes France turned away satisfied of its being empty. It was yet too dark to study the ground for marks of returning horses, and the corral offered no solution to the problem, since an indeterminate number of ponies had been held there over a period of days and the crew's mounts, if they had been recently turned in, were mingled with the rest. The barn, being at the far end of the yard, he dismissed for the moment and turned to the main house.

The door was closed though he remembered leaving it open earlier in the evening. Possibly the Chinaman had closed it. Approaching the porch he studied the flanking windows with considerable care and, on the verge of walking up the steps, recoiled with a feeling of dissatisfaction. It was first break of day—a time for people to be rising. By all rights the Chinaman should have a light in the kitchen, and the fact that there was none set France definitely on edge. He turned sharply and started to circle the house. At this moment he heard the Oriental squeak out a wailing phrase. The door opened and a tall figure stood in it. "Now!" he yelled. "Take what you got comin'!"

France dropped like a rock beside the porch. A bullet broke the air over his head. A second splintered the boards within a foot of his cheek, and a third, slashing through the flooring and siding, shook the loose earth into his face. He hooked his gun over the board ends and took chance aim. The aggressor—whom France had recognized as being Whiskers again—had jumped back and ceased firing, but his excited bellow rang through house and yard. "Get around him, you leadfoots! Flank him! Knock him down—rip it into him! He's finished right now! I got him so's he can't back clear!"

Another bullet splintered the boards and went ricocheting with a thrumming sound. The rest of the bunch were literally obeying orders. France heard them clumping around the house from either direction. In such a situation he was doomed to be whipsawed and killed. Still out of sight he ducked a yard farther along the ground, lifted his head to the level of the porch flooring and flung a bullet into the black rectangle of the door. At the same instant he vaulted up to the porch and lunged forward, still firing, fanning Whiskers out of the aperture, disturbing the man's aim.

A jet of flame spat at him, touched his sleeve. The man's voice, trembling with passion, taunted him to cross the sill. In a single flash of thought John France saw his chances slimming down. The rest of the group were rushing for the front porch pell-mell and in another moment would be upon him. It was up to him to move—and with that conviction he sent a shot ahead of him, jammed into the darkness of the room and set it a-roaring with a raking, plunging fire. Not until the hammer fell on a blank did it occur to him this room was silent with death. Standing with his face to the doorway France saw in the pale half-light the torso of Whiskers sprawled across it.

He stepped back, ripping the spent shells out of the gun cylinder and thumbing fresh ones in. The others were smashing bullets into the front wall of the house with a headlong fury. The window panes shattered one by one. Pressing against a wall he made out a man scurrying across the yard to gain the protection of the porch foot. He laid a shot close enough to check the fellow and spin him around for more shelter. Then, hearing a swiftly whispered parley passing between the remaining two crouched out there beside the steps, France tiptoed to the back door, skirted the house and came up alongside. They seemed to have suspected he might try such a movement for they were sidling off in the direction of the bunkhouse as he turned the porch corner. He followed them with a fresh attack as they broke into a running retreat. Pausing to go in and get the dead rustler's gun and fill it, France zigzagged across the yard. They were beyond the bunkhouse and at the far end of the cleared area. He lost them for a little while and then they flashed out, a-saddle, and cut for the creek. All three of them opened on him, but the distance and the light and the movement of their ponies sent all slugs wide of the mark.

He stopped, hearing one of the trio call for a return. "Ride the whelp down! He's got Deuce!" A swift opposition silenced him and they splashed over the creek and up the hill. He heard them stop and a long call floated down to him.

"France, this is the worst night's work you ever did! You got Deuce and you laid out Slip LaFleur temporary, yonder by the beef. Just keep this in your bonnet—you're a walkin' dead man from now till the bullet cuts you down."

He didn't answer, and they raced upward, the sound of their retreat presently dying. A strange quiet filled the meadow. He circled the barn to where their horses had been standing. There was one left—which would belong to the dead man in the house. One dead and three fleeing. Evidently the fifth of the original crew had been the Slip LaFleur they said he had pinked when making his getaway from the rustlers. So deciding, he walked back to the house to find the Chinaman holding a lamp above Whiskers—Deuce Evernight.

"Poor devil," muttered France. "That's all he's got to show for being somebody else's hired dummy."

The Chinaman's yellow face never turned a line. "Damn good all light. He all time say I bad cook. I bes' cook in countlee. No good—no good, him Deuce. All bad. Now you come bleakfas' befo' it get cold."

France sprang to the door. The reverberation of a fast traveling cavalcade swelled through the morning air. A string of riders bunched at the front gate, hauled it open and rode through. The nasal challenge of Slim Hillis hailed the house twenty yards distant. "Hello there, France. What's wrong?"

"Come ahead," said France. "Nothing wrong now. It's all over."

"I sort of figured you'd have some grief with that bunch," explained Hillis, slipping from the saddle, "so I started early. Heard the firin' and poured steel into these hay burners. Then his quick eye took in the broken glass and the prone figure of Deuce Evernight inside the door. "Great jumpin' jackrabbits, it looks like a revolution struck this joint! That Evernight? Dead? Uh-huh."

A moment's silence fell over the party. Hillis studied France with a queer intentness. Then he nodded.

86

"You'll do. No pleasure knockin' the light out of anybody, but you didn't start it and they've got it comin'. Glad to see you ain't the kind to get buck fever. Didn't think you would. This business ain't over by a long shot. It's just started, and it won't end until this county's cleaned up or we're all chased to hell and gone out of the state."

The Chinaman swore in his own language and added a line of impatient English. "Dam' all time trouble. Las' night I cook fo' six, feed five. Now no got bleakfas' only one an' come seven. All time trouble. By golly, you come get coffee."

Breakfast was over. The new crew had placed the dead Deuce Evernight in a bedroom and spread a blanket over him. Out in the front yard France had drawled out the night's story and now was inspecting the men Hillis had brought in. A faint smile broke the corners of his mouth.

"Well, Slim, if these boys had come up to my gate alone I don't believe I'd have had nerve to hire any one of them. They look kind of tough."

They were oddly assorted riders, none of them young and one with silver in his mane. They had a settled, weathered look about them and around their faces were many down-slanting lines. It took but one glance to see they had cut their teeth on the old-time range and shed most of them as well. And they studied France as carefully and noncommittally as he studied them. Hillis grinned.

"I know these boys. I'm just a kid whippersnapper alongside of the bunch. But you can bank your last nickel on the fact they know all the tricks in the game, every wrinkle and sand furrow in this country and the pedigree of every jasper livin' within forty miles of the Circle IF front gate. I know 'em. From left to right—Deal Durham, Big Jones, Fred Oatman, Canary Ellensburg and Mexico Sperry. Gents, your new boss. And now, we better rope out some fresh horses and hit the trail. You said they rustled that stock north from Cottonwood Meadows, huh? Yeah, well I know about where we'll find it."

"In case they haven't pushed the stuff on since then."

"No," decided Hillis, "they won't. Their hand's been tipped and they'll leave that bunch of critter's severely alone. And they won't try any daylight gunplay either. It ain't their style. We'll fog the beef back down where it belongs."

"Good idea," agreed France. "After that we'll have to buckle into the job of rounding up the rest of the brand and seeing how we stand. I'll get another pony and string along."

"We won't need you," said Hillis. "Won't be a particle of trouble to it. You better get a little sleep."

France considered the matter. "Well, I'll have to go to town today with some mail. Also have to tell the sheriff and the coroner about Evernight. Maybe I'll just catch up a couple of winks."

"Uh-huh," muttered Hillis and was thoughtful.

"Don't be careless when you go to town, and don't let Poco Finn rib you into anything, either. He's sheriff. He's something more than sheriff, likewise, which I won't mention in front of polite company. Maybe you better wait till we come back and let me ride along. You got to remember that from this minute on there ain't a Circle IF man that's got a good bill of health in these parts. I want to impress that on your judgment. It's a war between this outfit and a gang that's got Crowheart tied and gagged. War to the finish."

"I think I'm safe enough in going to town," drawled France.

"All right. You're the boss." Hillis led his outfit away. There was confusion in the corrals as they changed horses. France watched them ride up the trail and then rolled into bed for a short sleep.

The Chinaman slipped noiselessly to the open bedroom door, gripping a meat cleaver in his skinny hand. He stood there looking down on France's long body with the perfect impassivity of his race. Slipping softly away he crossed to the front porch, stared up into the timber and settled into a rocker, pushing himself to and fro as he watched.

## CHAPTER VI

France woke with a start and swung off the bed to land in stocking feet like a cat. He had heard a foreign sound in the house and it acted on him like an alarm clock. But when the sound came again he relaxed and reached for his boots. It was a woman's voice calling from the other end of the main room.

"Sleeping in the day? Do you know dinner is smoking on the table for you, John France?"

He came out. Louise Drood, trim in a man's riding clothes, stood by the front door smiling at him. It struck him all of a sudden that she was prettier than he had first decided her to be. Not being overly observant insofar as woman's dress was concerned he didn't realize she had changed her outward appearance from top to bottom. Like any other girl who had looked long in the mirror Louise Drood knew what colors subdued and at the same time accentuated her charm; and so now his attention was arrested, as she meant it to be, by the picture she made. From the rounding, compact fullness of her little shoulders and small white throat to the jet and gleaming hair done in woman's mysterious way upon her head she reminded John France of some brief and vivid flower bursting out of the bud. Her cherry lips were half parted. The rouge of inner excitement tinted her cheeks and her dark eyes held a provocative directness that was so much a part of her. And yet France seemed to see in them a touch of wistfulness as if the halves of her nature were warring for possession.

"Ready to eat?" she demanded, breaking the silence with her usual forthright manner. "You better be. I shoved your Chinese aside by main force and cooked this meal myself. Never knew any man's cooking yet

90

that tasted better than so much wrapping paper soaked in grease."

"Well, now—" began France.

"Oh, don't let it upset you. Everybody around Crowheart knows I'm apt to do absolutely anything that enters my head. You've got a look in your eyes that means shave and wash. Know it by heart. All right, run along, and I'll have a walk around the yard."

There was no mistake about the meal. When he came into the dining room, fresh and fit, it was on the table and the girl sitting across from his place. "Eat," she murmured. "It's for you, not me. I only drink coffee at noon."

He was still puzzled, and for a moment he studied her thoughtfully. She had a chance to see then more clearly those angles of a man's face that serve as infallible channel marks of character. He was more habitually sober minded than she had first guessed, and capable of far more stubborn resistance. Sitting quiet, straight in her chair, a faint quirk of lip corners to indicate a suppressed smile, she watched him settle down to the meal. Watched him with a quiet possessiveness.

"Did I look like this proposition upset me?" he drawled, lifting his fork. "Well, maybe it did. I don't recall this ever happening to me before."

It is a weakness of mine," she said, "to want to do things other people haven't done. Of course, I make a fool of myself sometimes. That's part of the bargain."

"Set it down that this isn't one of those times," was his quick reply.

91

"Thanks. When I do crazy things I pick my victims carefully. I don't make mistakes—often."

The last word was so definitely sad that he shot a swift glance over the table; but she shook her head, smiling again. "You go on and eat. I'm just talking to cover up my tracks."

But after a long while she asked him a very slow and casual question. "I suppose you have fired your crew?"

He put himself instantly on guard. She was a Drood and, willingly or otherwise, a part of the machine set against him. "They re gone," said he with a shortness he instantly regretted.

"Do you think they'll come back?"

"It depends, I guess, on how bad they want their pay. They didn't stop to get it."

And still in the same quiet tone she answered her own question. "They will come back, John France."

"I won't ask you how you happen to know that," was his slow rejoinder. "And it might be better if you drew the line on what you tell me."

"So you've discovered already what the Drood name stands for?"

He turned so somber at betraying his knowledge that she lifted a white hand with a swift, interrupting move. "I'm not pumping you! I'm not running down here to spy on you for my father! Don't you suppose I have a mind? Don't you suppose I can see and hear and guess? This country is nothing but a whispering gallery and I catch all the echoes."

He relaxed. The sincerity of the girl was too plain to be doubted. "Well, I'm sorry."

"Why should you be? You're on a trigger edge. You've got a right to challenge me. Only—I hope the time will come when you won't. But that crew will come back. Why, I can shut my eyes and almost tell you where everybody within ten square miles stands at this minute. I grew up with this stuff in my head. Pop made a boy out of me. He's said I could track a snake over a mile of lava rock and it is almost true. It's the only world I've got."

"Like it?"

Her fist lying on the table dosed until the knuckles whitened. "I hate it! What chance have I got to be like a real woman? I don't even know how to be one! If I did I wouldn't be doing all the weird and skitty things that folks think are funny. I don't think they're funny. I think they're pathetic. It's no fun being raised like a man."

"You've got yourself wrong," decided France, finishing his coffee. "When you go home look in the mirror. It's a picture that ought to satisfy any man's idea of a woman."

She drew in her breath sharply. "You think so?" she murmured. "I'm glad to hear you say that. I told you I picked my victims carefully when I did crazy things. You know, I like men with yellow hair. Don't ask me how I know—but you were never in greater danger of losing your life than you are today. You shouldn't be here alone. You ought never to ride alone. You should keep Slim Hillis around, or some of the men he brought in this morning."

"How did you know that?" challenged France.

"I told you I was a regular Indian," she said, shrugging her shoulders. "Well—"

A rider came drumming along the yard and drew into the porch. Laurel Annison's clear voice hailed the house; then her quick step echoed in the room. Instantly Louise Drood's eyes clouded up, and a sultry, half-sullen expression fell over her face. France had only time to rise in the chair when Laurel stood in the dining room door.

"Well, the grapevine's been working again," she began, and then, seeing Louise Drood, cut the sentence short. There was a flash and a change in the tall girl's manner. "Oh, I see you have company. Hello, Louise. I guess we both pulled our pickets and strayed at the same time."

"Hello," murmured Louise and turned away. The scene made France extremely uncomfortable and so did Laurel Annison's queer glance toward him. Something prompted him to explain this atmosphere of family comfort.

"Now, I'm glad to have you visit my house," he said as casually as he could. "This country certainly believes in makin' a stranger feel at home. This lady," nodding at Louise, "has just treated me to a home cooked meal. It being noon, won't you draw a chair?"

"Thanks, no," murmured Laurel. "I really wouldn't intrude on previous company. You ought to enjoy your dinner. Louise is famed for being a good cook. But if you don't mind may I talk with you a moment?"

France nodded an apology to Louise and walked back to the front porch with Laurel Annison. "As I said," she said crisply, "the grapevine's been working again. I heard about some trouble last night. I wondered if anything had happened to you." Then she grew impatient with herself. "I seem to be getting awfully inquisitive over other people's business lately. Excuse me for horning into your affairs. But since you are a neighbor and I offered you my outfit whenever you needed help I thought I'd ride over and see if you wanted to borrow any of my men."

"There was a ride and an argument," he admitted. "I ran into a bunch of boys playing tag with some stock in that high meadow. So I just played along until they discovered me and chased me out."

"Cottonwood Meadow? That's your range and your stuff. Was that all that happened?"

"Complications set in," he drawled. "Thanks for the offer, but I've got Hillis and five good men on the job now."

She pursed her lips and looked thoughtfully down the yard. France, watching her, was struck by the immense difference in the two women. Laurel Annison was tall and sure and seemed never to have a moment's doubt of herself. There was a firmness about her that Louise Drood would never have. But . . .

"Well," she said, breaking into his thoughts, "I'll be riding along. The offer still stands. I knew that the hills would see trouble sooner or later but I didn't think it would come so quickly. Oh, I'm sorry to think of it! I can't see how it will end."

"Neither do I right now," agreed France, reaching for his tobacco. "But things can only come one at a time, and we'll fight it out on that line."

"Yes, that's your way," she answered and looked back at him. "Really, I didn't mean to break into company. You go back and finish your dinner. Louise is a pretty kid when she wants to be. You ought to consider yourself flattered at having her cook for you."

"Well, now—"

She was down the steps and into her saddle. "Please don't. You certainly have no reason to explain anything to me, have you? This is your house, John France." And she whirled away. Up along the slope the suppressed anger came out and she lectured herself severely. "So you get off your high horse and grow catty, Laurel Annison? After knowing him just one day! What a fool he must think I am! Why should it hurt me to see them sitting there as comfortable as man and wife? If he likes Louise's way of throwing herself at him I can't blame him. Pretty? I have never seen the little devil look sweeter. But she's not up to him. Never in a thousand years is she good enough for him. Why don't men see those things? I wish I knew. . . ."

She forced this out of her mind. "Every window glass on the front side of the place is broken. The wall was full of bullet marks and that stain on the floor by the door was fresh. I wish I could do something to help, but I can't! Something terrible is coming out of this! He's got courage to burn but I wish he was more careful of himself."

She had scarcely cleared the meadow before Louise Drood walked from the dining room and straight by France. She had changed in that small interval of time, the color gone from her face and eyes burning with a strange, clouded emotion. She looked at the wreckage made by the recent gunplay and the irregular stain on the floor that was Deuce Evernight's life blood. And her body trembled. A white hand touched France with a light, brushing glance. At that moment she was like a frightened, saddened child.

"You haven't realized," she whispered, "what I've been trying to tell you. I know! You're a marked man. You'll never take another step that isn't watched. Do you suppose, being a Drood, I would have come down here if it wasn't that serious? I shouldn't say it—but I do."

Louise ran to her horse and before France had a thought of replying she was gone through the front gate. Beyond it she veered to the left and raced around the far side of the ridge toward home—crying, swearing, running the whole range of tempestuous emotion, from a fury of anger to the other extreme of self-condemning humbleness.

France walked thoughtfully back to the roll-top desk and sat down. He drew out a sheet of paper and started to write a letter, but the events of the morning crowded everything else out of his mind, leaving him disturbed and uncertain. With men he was on sure ground, but these women left him completely up in the air and at the end of ten minutes the only conviction he had was that Laurel Annison went away with a show of temper and a false impression—the last thing in the world he wanted her to have.

"A fellow made a statement about women once," he mused. "I don't know who it was or what he said, but he certainly was right. Coming back to brass tacks, I've been warned three times in the last few hours. First Slim, then the Drood girl and next Laurel Annison. That seems to make it unanimous that I'm in trouble. Such being the case I guess I'd better play my hole card."

So deciding, he wrote and sealed the letter and went out for a horse. Coming by the house he called to the Chinaman that he would be home late and then struck south for Crowheart. All along the way he was plunged in thought that his habitual survey of the surrounding country was somewhat abated.

"I've got to take the aggressive," he thought. "If I hang back and let them do the attacking, I'll be nibbled to pieces. It's up to me to hit straight from the shoulder and keep on doing that until something drops. But I can see right now that six men isn't enough to do it. The odds are too strong."

Coming up to the butte that was split in half by the trail passing through, he stopped to study the rising walls on either side. "Not good revolver range from the top of that rock," he reflected. "But a man with a rifle could do a lot of damage. I ought to have brought mine. Too easy to get flanked and knocked down in this rolling country. Hereafter I'll put a boot under the saddle skirt and pack a thirty caliber."

But he rode straight through as he had done before and put the butte behind him. In the middle of the afternoon he came into Crowheart and stopped first at the postoffice. He bought a stamp for his letter and was on the point of giving it to the postmaster when something in the man's eyes—a glint of curiosity or a shifting expression—stopped his hand. The postmaster's fingers were even touching the letter when France drew it away.

"When will this go? Westbound."

"Makin' up the sack right now," said the postmaster and looked at his watch. "Be a train through in half an hour."

France pocketed the letter and turned away. The postmaster warned him that the sack was being closed in another ten minutes but France only nodded and walked out. His steps carried him up to Kidder's office. It was empty but he scarcely had time to turn around before he heard the gross-bodied lawyer heaving up the stairs.

"Saw you from the restaurant," said the lawyer and sank into his swivel chair with a grunt of relief. "Want somethin'?"

"I suppose you've got all of the ranch books and business papers," said France. "I'll need them now.

Also want you to introduce me to the bank."

"Your account's open at the bank," said the lawyer. "That's been straightened out from Omaha. But as for any of Ike's records, I ain't got a one. Fact is I didn't find nothin' of importance in his desk."

"Stolen?"

Kidder pursed his little dab of a mouth. "Wouldn't go so far as to say that. Ike was a hand to carry all his affairs in his head. Probably didn't have no records in writin'."

"Unfortunately that isn't true," was France's dry rejoinder. "The will distinctly mentions records that I would find. And I haven't found them. Where are they?"

Kidder twisted. "Well, I ain't got 'em."

"Somebody has," snapped France. "Clever move. Without the records I have absolutely no idea of how much livestock I'm supposed to find. The people who are trying to freeze me out of the country understand that pretty well. But if they think they've got me stopped they're due for a surprise. I'll cut every bunch of beef in this country to locate my strays. I've been at the business long enough to know all the tricks."

Kidder's interest mounted. "You mean you'll ride everybody's range to look for your brands?"

"Put it stronger than that. I'll have a man at every roundup within twenty miles and I'll stop and inspect every herd of beef that starts for the railroad."

"That's unfriendly," grunted Kidder.

"Not in an honest country," retorted France. "It's my

100

legal right. Where I come from it is quite customary."

Kidder's hand dived into a drawer for a bag of chocolates. He up-ended the bag at his mouth and the candy poured down. Presently he muttered, "You ain't green enough to suppose anybody's goin' to drive a beef steer with your brand on it openly to market."

"I expect to find some blotched brands," stated France baldly.

"Hah. You got a job proving a brand's been changed in this country."

"Thanks for the information," drawled France, and at that juncture he had Kidder completely analyzed. "I'm glad to know the officials are crooked."

"Hold on, I didn't say that!" bellowed Kidder and treated himself to a display of anger. "What the hell right have you got to come in my office and twist my words around in such a manner? You better back up. I could have you thrown in the jug for six months for makin' a crack like that. It's defamation of character and contempt of court."

"What side of the fence are you on?" challenged France. "Let's get that straight. I want to know when accounting time comes."

"Suggestin' I'm crooked?" bellowed Kidder. "Why, you—" But he never finished the sentence. Instead his pig eyes turned away from France's level gaze and he crossed his fat fingers on his paunch. The anger, being the kind that a lawyer often develops for trial purposes and effects, died away. "Bad policy for a stranger like you to shoot off your face so sudden. You ain't got a scrap of evidence to sustain a blamed word you've said to me.

"In the first place my reputation's open to view any time, anywhere. In the second place, your threat of an accountin' sounds like a man tryin' to bet a pair of deuces against a king full. What the hell have you got to force an accountin' with? If you think that sounds like I'm crooked, help yourself to the mustard. Bein' a lawyer I'm tryin' to steer you straight, which you need some bad. I know this country. It's a good, honest one and your remarks as to rustlin' and brand blotchin' are both previous and unnecessary. Don't ask me to help if you land in trouble."

France rose, hearing the whistle of the approaching train. "That doesn't seem to jibe with your previous statement to me about this being a hard country for a pilgrim to tackle. Guess you've changed your mind, or had it changed for you. It is none of my concern, only I want to repeat that I'm out for cold turkey and if I find my meat there may be such a thing as folks in the background. You lawyers call it accessory after the fact. And don't be too sure I haven't got anything better than a pair of deuces."

He walked out and toward the depot as the train pulled in. He had made some rather rash statements, not because he was temporarily inclined that way but because he wanted to throw a scare into Kidder and, through Kidder, let the other side know he was on the warpath. Keep the rustlers guessing, force the issue.

He walked forward to the mail car and handed his

letter personally to the clerk at the door of the car just as the postmaster threw up Crowheart's sack. The postmaster stared glumly at France.

"What's the idea? Ain't my handlin' good enough for your mail?"

"Nothing personal," drawled France. "Just wanted to think the letter over before I sent it." The clerk of the mail car laughed and closed the door. The train moved away. France returned to the street and, opposite the stable, heard somebody bearing down from behind. He swung to see the sheriff, Poco Finn, coming up at a fast walk.

"Say, France," called the sheriff, "I want to talk with you. Heard they was some trouble up your way. Some shootin'. That right?"

"How did you hear?" countered France.

"I hear things," was the sheriff's mysterious answer. "What I want to say is this county is peaceable, and we don't allow no gunplay. If they's been serious trouble I'll have to hold you to account."

"Got a coroner here?"

"Coroner? No. We got a doctor good enough but he ain't in town. Why?"

"Then you'd better ride out to the ranch with me and see Deuce Evernight. He's dead. You can bring him back with you in the livery stable rig I drove away yesterday."

"Killed?" asked the sheriff, not showing surprise. His attention sharpened and he took a step backward.

"The boys wanted to see how good my nerves were

103

and slung some lead. Deuce got in the road."

"Whose road?" challenged Finn.

"Didn't the little bird tell you that when he told you the rest of it?" was France's gentle query.

The sheriff shifted weight, feeling his way cautiously around the subject. "I heard a different story. Heard you picked a quarrel deliberate with Deuce and drilled him cold."

"Who said that?" demanded France.

"Never mind who said it. 'Twas said. I'll say again I don't tolerate that sort of monkey business around Crowheart. It looks fishy to me. We ain't had a smell of powder smoke nor the sound of so much as a firecracker in these parts for six months or better. Kind of funny a killin' should happen within a day of your arrival. I'll have to hold you."

"You're not holdin' anybody till you go out and see the layout for yourself," retorted France. "Don't get too anxious. I'm starting home now. Come along."

"We-ell," muttered Poco Finn, and thought about it in his slow, flat-footed manner. France, never allowing his attention to stray from the official for a single instant, tried to fathom Finn's motives. Judging from Slim Hillis' casual hint, Finn was bought and kept by the rustler ring. Possibly the man was acting under orders now; possibly he was acting under his own initiative. But from his uncertainty, France rather believed Finn's obtuse mind was grappling with a problem that somebody else hadn't yet solved for him. In other words Finn was without orders. At any rate he finally nodded in a half surly manner. "All right. I'll go along and see. But I'll probably have to bring you back. Wait a minute while I go to the office."

"I'll keep you company that far," said France and fell in step with the sheriff. Finn seemed impatient. When he reached the courthouse steps he halted and then slapped a hand to his thigh. "Oh, let it go. I'll tend to that when I come back. Here's my horse. I'll ride along while you go ahead to get yours."

France stood still till the sheriff rode down the street in front of him and then followed toward the postoffice where his own pony waited. The sheriff swung to the far side of the street to intercept a gangling man in a floppy vest, and France, moving with outward casualness, got into his saddle and reined around to command this scene. The sheriff bent swiftly and passed a phrase to the townsman, who nodded and walked away. France, half a glance on each of these fellows, waited. Then the sheriff rode abreast of him and together they cantered out of town. In the interval of jockeying France had shifted about the sheriff until his gun side was nearest him. Finn's irritation grew pronounced and finally broke through.

"What the hell's all this cat-walkin' for? Think somebody's tryin' to auger you from behind your back?"

"In my country," drawled France, "my folks were honest as a rule but pretty careful."

"Well," stated Finn heavily, "you can put it down that when I want you I won't come up from behind.

I'll walk straight in your direction and call for your gun like a gentleman. That's my style. I ain't found a man yet I was afraid to brace and you ain't no exception to the rule."

"Spoken like a sport," applauded France, which was a piece of polite fiction on his part. Finn hadn't spoken it like a sport at all. The man was upset, morose and a little uneasy. For a mile or better he held his peace, attention darting from France to the country on either side. And then he began talking again.

"You may be high ace in your own country, wherever that is, but you can't come down here and raise hob with law-abidin' folks. Deuce Evernight was a fine fellow. In case I find you shot him because he was a little dubious about lettin' you settle down on the ranch without due credentials I'll sure have to hold you. Deuce had a right to question your presence on that ranch. Takin' care of it was his responsibility and he had to be mighty strict with strangers."

"I expect he had his orders on the subject all right," said France.

The sheriff didn't like the sound of the phrase and he challenged it. "What you mean by that?"

"Just what I said."

"Yeah? Well, I want to tell you somethin', Mr. France. You ain't sittin' in a good spot with this country. When news drifted in about the shootin' scrape they was some ugly things said about you in Crowheart. You ain't got public sentiment with you a-tall. Strangers can't expect to take liberties around here. We wash our own dirty dishes without askin' outside help. I got to do my duty and I don't want no pullin' on the rope from you."

"That depends on which way you try to lead me," was Frances laconic reply.

The sheriff relapsed to a moody silence and increased the pace of travel. France noted that the man kept up a vigilant inspection of the land ahead and for that matter he, too, watched his flanks with an increased care, though he seemed to be looking straight to the front. Presently the butte bore down upon them. The sheriff craned his neck to survey the ragged rock brow and he threw another warning over his shoulder. "I trust you ain't fool enough to work any tricks on me, France. It'd go hard on you."

"That's my worry, not yours. I've been shot at by experts. But if it's troubling your head we'll just ride through this slash side by side. If anybody wants to pot you they'll have to aim at me. And the other way around likewise."

They entered the mouth of the small canyon abreast of each other. The sunlight fell off. The echo of the horses' hoofs striking the hard underfooting rang along the walls and came sharply back. In the semi-shade Poco Finn's dark cheeks seemed taut from temple to chin and his dusky eyes kept rolling upward. He was distinctly nervous and he had trouble keeping his horse beside that of France. The latter fixed his glance straight to the front and cantered on. A little past midway, a rock, half as large as a hat, rocketed down the steep slope and broke into fragments. Finn began to swear. The horse beneath him pitched and hauled aside and ahead.

Precisely at that instant when the men were separated by a matter of yards the calm of the canyon was shattered by the flat report of a gun on the west rim above. France felt the touch of that bullet like the tap of a finger. Looking down he saw a ragged, foot-long seam in the cloth of his right trouser leg and blood welling slowly along the path of broken skin. Poco Finn's horse had either bolted or was given free rein for the sheriff was racing madly on out of the trap, yelling at the top of his lungs. France flung his mount as far into the left wall as the shale rock would permit and swung to look above. He saw the muzzle of a gun veering around to command this sharper angle, and also the brim of a man's hat.

With that picture in his head he slashed the horse with his spurs and shot through the canyon, slipping himself down along the near stirrup. The second bullet, whining through the still air, brought up small clots of earth nearby. The third—seeming to come after an interminable period of careful waiting—sent a hot breath against his cheek and went on to rut a furrow in the ground. There were no more. He flashed out of the defile and around a protecting cornice of the butte.

Never checking speed, he curved with the butte to gain the long slope of its westward side and thus ascend it. Looking around he saw the sheriff a good

two hundred yards away and standing behind the protecting side of his horse. He yelled at the official to
come on but there was no answering call or movement—and France knew then that Finn, having
guessed the identity of the ambusher, was putting himself out of the fight. All this might have been pre-
arranged at the moment the sheriff stopped in town to
pass word to that gangling townsman. At any event
Poco Finn was letting the dice roll.

The sheer side lowered into the westward roll of the
butte; France threw his pony hard around and took the
grade at a harsh pace. He could see a matter of four or
five hundred feet up along that incline to where a
rock-strewn parapet marked the butte's leveling top.
Gun out, he crisscrossed the sage and loose areas of
shale. On up he forced the pony, feeling the labor of
the beast's muscles and barrel. Of a sudden, a hundred
feet away, a rider broke through the parapet and
started down the slope with reckless speed, rifle held
free in one hand.

It was Big Ben Golloway and France saw the
gunman's sweaty face contort and blacken. The man
brought his horse about with a cruel wrench of effort
and threw his gun into a loose aim. France sent a shot
across the closing space. Golloway flung the rifle
from him, returned to the top of the parapet and disappeared. When France broke through to the level
area he found Golloway leaping from the saddle and
running in awkward strides toward a patch of high
boulders. France forced his pony onward until Gol-

loway dived behind the rock, and then he left his horse in one sprawling jump and flattened himself against the ground. A revolver shot passed above him.

The distance between was approximately fifty feet. The upstanding rocks had interstices here and there through which Golloway could fire, and France, half blinded by the streaming salt sweat cropping out of his forehead, knew himself to be in a bad fix. There was nothing to do but run for it. Rising, he plunged toward the rock, veering from side to side. Golloway, evidently, was changing positions for he didn't challenge France until the latter had come within twenty feet. Then France saw the man, standing openly on the far end of one of the interstices, lift his gun to take a careful, cold aim. France whipped a bullet into the aperture. Golloway flinched and his own bullet went wide. Dropping back and aside he took a pot-shot. France veered again and then was flat against a boulder, on the far side of which he could hear Golloway breathing laboriously.

"Stand out in the open with me, you chicken-livered son!" yelled Golloway.

France slipped to his right to round the rocks. He skipped across another aperture, losing the sound of Golloway's breathing. Stepping softly he crawled onward. Once, thinking he heard a brush of boots against the flinty ground, he flattened his back to the rock and looked either way, but he saw nothing. Golloway was playing this game of deadly tag with him. There was still another opening he had to pass before reaching the west flank of the stone outcrop. Reaching to the ground for a rock the size of an egg, he pitched it over the barrier and toward the east. When it fell he slipped past the opening and at last arrived at one end of the outcrop. He lifted his hat and put it before him. Nothing happened. Hooking himself around the corner he approached Golloway's side on tip-toe, reached another corner and with a swift backstep, cleared it. The gunman was not to be seen.

France held his place a moment, dashing the sweat out of his eyes with a swift rub of his free forearm. His nerves were singing like taut wires against a high wind yet his pulse was small and slow and all his senses were tuned up to catch the least stray sound along this hot, still table top. Either Golloway had circled the far end of the rocks or he was concealed in one of the apertures, hoping to out-wait and wear down his antagonist. Standing thus and debating the moves open to him, France suddenly picked up a break in the droning air, a sound once heard never forgotten and never mistaken—the dry, deadly rhythm of a snake rattling. It came from the side of the rocks France had just left and it meant that the proximity of man had disturbed the rattler out of his sunning. Golloway was over there.

He stepped farther back from the rocks and jumped to the left. Down the length of the line of boulders, Golloway stood with his whole body crouched in an arc, facing France, gun leveled. He had been retreating but he froze in his tracks, yelled madly and opened up with his sixgun. France heard the blast of those shots as if they were far away, and then the running-in reply of his own gun. He felt the piece kicking against his wrists and the smell of powder smoke rose to his nostrils. Golloway still stood untouched. France himself felt no hit, and a distant, cool impulse told him to close up the space. Moving forward, he was swept by a fighting fury that boiled out the last shred of scruple or sympathy. His will commanded him to smash down and destroy this man who stood for the forces leagued against him. And at that moment John France was the gunman type, pure and simple.

Golloway shifted perceptibly. The firing seemed to be over. Silence returned to the table top and crowded down. Golloway, mouth wide apart and every muscle giving way, pitched forward in a bucking motion to the ground, sightless eyes staring aside to where the gleaming length of a rattlesnake slid sinuously off to safety.

France stared at the dead man, and then he turned abruptly on his heel and strode back to his horse. He galloped down the slope and around the butte, aiming at Poco Finn who sat motionless in the saddle. The sheriff made a furtive move of his arm but stopped it suddenly when he had a clearer view of France's features, still astir with destructive rage. He waited sullenly.

"If I thought you were a part of that rig-up," said France, choking back his anger, "I'd strip you down and rawhide the life out of you. When will you fools learn to leave me alone? Have I got to turn killer and clean up the country?"

"Who was it?" Finn asked sullenly.

France's gray eyes narrowed down on the sheriff. "In case you don't know, it was Golloway. If you're so set on keeping peace in the country, why was it you lagged back?"

"I ain't bustin' into any traps," growled Finn. Presently, feeling the cold hostility of the other man boring through him, he cried, " 'Fore Gawd, man, this was sudden an' unexpected to me!"

Let it be like that in the future as well," France said. "Now march in front of me to the ranch. When you drive back with Evernight you can stop and give a dead man fit company. Any objections?"

Finn shook his head.

## CHAPTER VII

Ten miles southeast of the Circle IF and three mornings later there was another conference of rustlers. Crossjack Drood had ridden over from a small roundup along the meadows of the Crazy Girl where he was gathering in some of his drift. Shortly after, Poco Finn cut across the rolling terrain from the direction of Crowheart. And as the two of them waited in the small depression, morosely silent, Al McQuarter made his appearance from the north. In contrast with

Drood's air of moody restlessness and Poco Finn's plainly worried manner, McQuarter was smiling and serene.

He was not a big man—both the others stood above him and were much heavier in bulk—and he always managed to groom himself well. A fresh neckpiece fluttered in the small breeze. His hair flashed in the light when he raised his hat to wipe the dust from his forehead. In a country that looked up to physical strength it was a significant fact that Al McQuarter's less than average size and his almost foppish habits were never mentioned in jest. And people never presumed to trade on his gay and friendly manner, for they knew what uncanny power of reflex and speed and directness was his. They had seen him split the edge of a playing card at a greater distance than the run of them were able to hit a quart pail.

"Good mornin', gentlemen," he said. "You boys sure seem light-hearted about somethin'. Ever seen the beginnin' of a finer day? By Jo, this is weather that makes a fellow glad to be above the sod."

"Come off," Drood growled. "The weather ain't got a thing to do with our affairs. We're all a-settin' on a mess of sharp tacks and it's time to do somethin' about it. Up till now, Al, you ain't done nothin' but sit back and give orders that's got us in more grief. Spread yourself and take an active hand."

"What seems to be biting you most?" asked McQuarter, rolling a cigarette. His quick glance passed over the two. It was at such times that the

114

genial manner betrayed itself by a certain frosty calculation in the blue eyes.

"You know what France has been doin'?" Drood said. "He's been scourin' his range with a fine tooth comb. And he's got his crew split up, pokin' into this place and that one. I can't cross a square mile of ground without findin' solitary tracks cuttin' in front of me. He's watchin' us better'n we're watchin' him. I can't tell when I'll run into him or where. This business makes me nervous. We got to take the reins and drive."

"We ain't done a thing since he laid Golloway in the dust," added Finn. "Why?"

"Because," explained McQuarter, inhaling smoke, "I wanted to see what he'd do if left alone. We prodded him pretty hard right off the bat and naturally he clawed back. I figured that if we just played possum he might quit scrappin' and mind his own business—in other words that he'd write off his losses in stock and forget about it and go ahead as a good neighbor."

"Well," broke in Drood, "he ain't. He's after his lost beef. He ain't the kind to take a loss in a handsome manner. He's runnin' around this country so frequent that we ain't got the privacy of a cat eatin' supper among a pack of dogs."

"Supposin'," Finn wanted to know, "he had turned peaceable and not tried to hit back? What of it?"

"In said case," murmured McQuarter, "I might have let him alone. We've almost got our profits out of his place and we could afford to leave him build up until he was sweet enough for another stingin'. Funny thing is, I'm a little uncertain. Some ways I like that fellow."

"Uh-huh," grumbled Drood. "But he ain't goin' to let us alone and we're a pack of fools to give him room enough to uncover us. That won't do."

"Correct," returned McQuarter. "Matter of fact, he should have been jailed after Evernight and Golloway went down. That's an easy way out. We could railroad him quick as a flash. Our own jury, judge and all."

"Simple to state," was Poco Finn's reluctant admission. "I tried to arrest him—but the durn fool ain't reasonable thataway. He's a fightin' man. If you got any sort of good idea on trappin' him into jail, though, I'll guarantee to keep him there till he rots."

"A trick it will have to be," admitted McQuarter. "He knows better than to put his foot outside of Crowheart alone. I want to tell you something—John France is no kid in the woods. He can give you boys cards and spades and still win points enough to make game. He's as tough as scrap iron."

"Don't have to tell me that," said Finn and pulled his shoulders together. "You ought to seen that gent's fightin' face when he come back from slaughterin' Golloway. Give me the chill, no denyin' that. I packed Evernight and Golloway back to town and I know France's ability. What made Golloway try to pot the fellow, anyhow?"

Drood and McQuarter exchanged swift glances that Finn never observed. "It was his own affair," said

McQuarter and let it go at that.

"Well, he went after poor Golloway like a wildcat goin' up a tree. Walked right into Golloway's fire. You fellows is foolish if you leave him play around loose. I'm tellin' you."

Drood suddenly swung on McQuarter. "So you think he's too much for Finn and me? How about yourself? Afraid of him? I see you ain't movin' in his direction very sudden."

McQuarter's serenity diminished. He ground the cigarette's hot tip beneath his fingers. "I can't quite make up my mind what's best to do. But if I ever start personally after him I'll walk up to the gentleman and put a pair of bullets in his heart before he knows I've drawn. That's flat.

"Don't throw it up to me. You gentlemen know what I'm capable of doing, if I've got to do it. So far I don't see the necessity. He's not that dangerous. The thing is to trick him into Crowheart and jail him. Easiest way to accomplish the trick is to go out and arrest one of his men. He'll come in then to protect his interests. You'd better get three or four men around Crowheart for such an emergency and keep them on watch."

"Still keepin' yourself out of the picture?" said Drood, half sneering.

"My policy," agreed McQuarter with so lifeless a drone that Drood jerked up his head. "But," went on McQuarter, "we'll have to pull him and his outfit out of the picture pretty soon. We can't have them spying to the northward. There's a shipment of beef due on the road right away. Have you cleaned his brands out of your own stuff, Drood?"

"Yeah, and all the poor blotches as well," said Drood. "I ain't takin' no chances. I got all that stuff in a separate bunch hid well in the hills. Sooner we get it off our hands the better. That's why I say we got to humble him before he discovers where his stuff went. Once he finds out—good night."

"Good night for him," amended McQuarter. "If he ever does find our back trail I will go kill him."

Drood's temper gave way. "Hell, all you do is talk, talk, talk! Then push somebody else into the shootin'! Yeah, I know you say you handle your end of the deal, which is to supply the market for the stuff we rustle, and so on and so forth. But it ain't enough for me! You're clear and I'm up to my neck in trouble! I'm the fall guy if France breaks through and finds out what's happenin'. Fact is he knows now I was hooked with Golloway in some kind of a deal, and that puts me in the light. I'm sick of it! Either we get France in forty-eight hours or I'll throw every head of his stock back where it belongs and wash my hands of the whole mess!"

Finn backed away to be out of the quarrel. McQuarter's blue eyes stared relentlessly at Drood. A whitening cast came over his blond features—the mark of that inner temper he loved to keep under cover. But, watching Drood, he shifted his attack to a different point. So, in a slow, slurring voice he struck back.

"Do you know, Drood, what the common talk is around the country? Your Louise girl's been in France's house three times in the last four days. She'd stay there longer if—"

"You lie!" yelled Drood, as black as thunder. "I'll kill the man who makes that statement! Swallow that—"

McQuarter shifted; his elbows lifted imperceptibly. But Drood had passed the point of caution.

"Swallow that, you filthy hog!"

"Now listen," said McQuarter, soothing the man, "You don't suppose I'm sayin' it to insult you? If I had a daughter I'd want to be told a thing like that. Soften up, Crossjack, I'm speakin' as a friend."

"It's a damned lie!"

McQuarter swung on Finn. "What about it, Poco? You tell him."

"Shucks," protested Finn, "why should I be talkin' out of turn? It ain't my affair."

Of a sudden Drood turned hard. "What do you know?" he asked Finn, suppressing his rage.

"It's talk," admitted Finn reluctantly. "Fact is, it's more'n talk. She's been seen goin' to and from Circle IF. She cooked France's breakfast four mornin's ago."

McQuarter reined his horse around. "I just wanted to drop the bug in your ear, Drood, so you could stop her from bein' foolish. I've got to hit back. Finn, you get some men organized in Crowheart for that job, then ride around and locate one of France's crew. "That'll draw France into the trap quick enough. So-long."

119

And he whirled over the rim, leaving Drood standing like one stricken dumb. Finn was slowly inching out of the wash in the opposite direction.

As McQuarter cut across the country in the direction of the Circle IF house a succession of swift thoughts went flashing through the cold, adroit brain. Whatever the handsome outward presence of the man was and notwithstanding the engaging smile he presented to the world, within he was all calculation and he thought only in terms of himself. There was not another man under the sky he either feared or loved or trusted a great deal. Early in life he had discovered the power of his personality and thenceforth he had put it to use to mask his illicit appetites. Like all supreme egoists he followed his star of fortune with a certain relentlessness of spirit and little consideration for anyone who stood in his way, and that star's frosty glitter was even warmer than his own heart.

He pushed other men in front of him, not because he was afraid but because they served to shelter him, because they were tools. So he had more or less urged Golloway on to death, balancing the possible results for the last degree of use he could find in them. And so now he had stabbed Drood in the man's most sensitive spot, fully believing that it would inflame him to the point of openly attacking France. And once again McQuarter weighed the results. France dead would mean the end of the fuss and no whisper of the killing would ever be attached to Al McQuarter. But if Drood fell in the fight, that meant the passing of another partner whose work was about done. By degrees Al McQuarter was breaking up the ring he himself had created. He would never be a scrupulous man nor an honest one, but he meant by one means or another to destroy the witnesses of his lawless past.

He was changing tactics with a certain cool ruthlessness and with, as usual, a greater aim in view. The aim now was the winning of Laurel Annison. All along his life there had been one person he had wanted, one woman he was willing to surrender certain of his liberties to. That was the single contradiction in the otherwise self-centered man. Knowing that she was too honest to accept a man with the least taint about him, or even to live with him after marriage if she discovered a red trail behind, McQuarter was bowing to the greatest of his desires and conforming to her code.

It was a further mark of his egoism that he believed he could utterly erase his past and keep it forever from her; that he could also conceal the basic qualities of his nature for the rest of his life. In that he was mistaken, for his previous relations with women had not warned him of feminine intuition. Nevertheless that was the belief upon which he based his change of plans.

But as he crossed the Circle IF range he was troubled by one figure that kept rising athwart his course—that of John France. Evernight and Golloway had gone down before the man's guns and outward from the Circle IF quarters emanated a steady, stubborn aggressiveness that would not be halted. Never for a moment had he misjudged France's character, but he was forced to admit that the man might become, overnight, the greatest antagonist he had ever thrown himself against.

These were the thoughts passing through the emotionless and delicate balance of his quick brain. There were others to deal with as well—Kidder, Finn, the punchers who knew his part, Louise Drood. He had a way for each of them. All that was left now was the disposition of the final bunch of rustled stock to the safe market up north. Then a winding up of the tag ends of the whole affair.

So, pleasant and urbane, McQuarter rode through the Circle IF gate and hailed the house. France came around from the corrals, a loose-jointed man with a calm and lazy manner at complete variance with the record behind him. He flipped an arm at McQuarter and drawled a slow greeting.

"Light and smoke."

But McQuarter shook his head, all the while trying to delve behind the barrier of the bronzed cheeks, trying to measure the man's farthest limit of ability. "No, I'm riding right on through home. Got my crew out on the spring work and shouldn't be loafing like I do. Just wanted to repeat that I want you to call on me for any help you might need."

"Thanks," said France, then seemed to be reminded of something. "By the way, I'm combing the country for drift. We'll be up your way in another day or two."

"Don't hesitate to drag my range from corner to corner," McQuarter answered. "I don't doubt you'll find some of your brands. They've scattered all over the map. I've already given my men instructions to bunch out anything they find that belongs to you."

"That's fine," agreed France and appeared to mean it. "Wanted you to know what I was doing. Don't wish for any hard feelings or misunderstandings."

"None between you and me," said McQuarter. "I want to get along with my neighbors. See you later." And he cantered across the creek and climbed the hill.

The trail to his own place turned right at the Cottonwood Meadows but he ignored it and kept going toward Laurel Annison's. Since the night he had abandoned her supper table he had not seen her, nor had she invited him back to make up the lost meal. Traveling on around the dizzy ledge of road, he felt a moment's doubt as to the girl and himself. He had fought hard for her favor but even yet the agreement between them was clouded with a trace of uncertainty on her part. Then his mind reverted to France—the slim newcomer's steadfast and level eyes, the long arms, the supple dexterity of the fingers. McQuarter had analyzed too many fighters in his career not to know the marks of ability.

"The gentleman," mused the blond McQuarter, "works on ball-bearing joints. There's a ripple to his muscles. He don't waste effort and he's packed full of energy that he can bring up all at once and smash out with. But I observe his gun ain't hung exactly right for his arm length. Even if he was as fast as me, which I doubt, that extra inch or so of play in his draw would be all the break I needed. Just a part of a second. Personally, I don't want to have to fight it out with him face to face. That would put me in a bad light with the country and with Laurel. It's best to cultivate him. A handsome rascal. . . ."

Turning a sharp bend of the road he saw Laurel Annison riding toward him at a fast clip, sitting in the saddle with a graceful laxity. He drew in and his questing glance, always searching for the smaller changes that revealed the true index of other people's feelings, discovered a quick sobering of Laurel's face. It was not like her to meet him with that manner of thoughtfulness, almost verging on embarrassment. Instantly she checked the pony's gallop and so approached him sedately. The fresh air of the morning had whipped a rosy color to her cheeks and about her was a free running vitality that added to the auburn beauty of her hair and the frank directness of her dark eyes. Al McQuarter never came near this girl without experiencing a lift of spirit and he did not conceal his pleasure now.

"Gosh," he drawled, "I'm lucky. You're a picture, Laurel."

"Seems like I've heard you say that before," she replied, smiling slightly.

"Doesn't hurt to repeat it. Women like to hear it."

"So it's taffy you're handing me, Al. Shame on you. Where bound?"

"To see you," was his prompt statement. "I was wonderin' if it was too late to express sentiments of regret for runnin' off from that meal."

"H'mm. I cooked a pie and I'd bought you a cigar. A woman spurned is nobody for a young fellow like you to treat lightly. But the pie was enjoyed anyhow and so was the cigar. Remember, you left a substitute."

McQuarter chuckled. "I think I made a mistake. First thing I know he'll be givin' me competition. Hope you didn't enjoy his presence too blamed much."

But she deserted her gay manner. "Al, he's a fine, strong gentleman. I—I couldn't have been blessed with a better neighbor. And he's fighting back. He's whipping the sneaking curs that have been trying to get him."

There was a distinct note of pride in her voice. She gave herself away. McQuarter's lids dropped and he studied the ground to avoid letting her see the swift fire that flamed through him. After a small silence he spoke slowly.

"You sound serious, Laurel."

She lifted her shoulders. "You know I'm not one to conceal what I think or feel, Al. That isn't my style."

"Then maybe it's serious, huh?"

"Why should you ask?"

"We-ell, I don't mean to presume, Laurel, but I thought I had that right. Am I mistaken?"

It was her turn to inspect the slight and wiry figure

before her and immediately she grew graver. "Is it that bad, Al?"

"Good Lord, if I was to lose out," said he huskily, "I don't know what I'd do."

She shook her head, a little sad. "You can never bank on a woman's heart. I have always been fair with you, haven't I? Haven't I always said that I liked you better than anyone, but still was just a little uncertain? We have always been pretty clear on that point. I couldn't have it any other way. And if there has been a change it isn't in your power or mine to stop it."

"Then there has been a change—and France has made it! Laurel, I've known you since we both were kids and I can't stand to see another man come in and take away—"

"Stop that!"

He drew a great breath and clenched the saddle-horn with a terrific pressure of fists. She had always known the power of his temper and always had admired him for keeping it so well controlled; but it made a distorted mask of his face now and pinched in his features cruelly. His eyes had changed color and were a-glitter with such a savagery of desire that it frightened her. A long moment later he won back to something like his old manner. "My fault, Laurel. I'm a blamed fool. Sorry. If you're just ridin' around maybe you won't mind my company."

"I was—just going to Cottonwood Meadows," she said, and found the lie distasteful. "But I'm turning back now. This had to come sooner or later. It hurts like the devil, I know, but it's better said and over with. I've got some work to do. See you later." He raised his hat and watched her swing away and turn right at the mailbox. Then he backtracked toward the meadow, the wreckage of his dreams afire in his body. "She was going down to see France! She lied to me! This is a chore I've got to do myself! If there ever was a doubt in my mind about that man it's settled now! I've got to kill him!"

At the meadow he swung off for his own place, but a few hundred yards north of the trail a shrewd thought occurred to him and he turned abruptly and put his horse beside a shoulder of rock. Twenty minutes later he heard a rider come pounding along from the west, from the direction of Annison's, and in a short while Freckles flashed past the rock, discovered McQuarter and turned in with a grunt of surprise.

"You seem on business," murmured McQuarter.

"Me?" said Freckles and tipped back his hat. "Say, I ain't nothin' but a doggone messenger boy between the Window Pane and Circle IF. Doggone, I get tired of it sometimes. And France was the dude that told Laurel he had a previous engagement! Hell."

"Got another message, huh?" inquired McQuarter.

"Yeah," agreed Freckles and then became taciturn. "Uh-uh."

"Never read those messages, I bet," suggested McQuarter softly.

"Who, me? What you take me for, Al? Course not."

"Don't look so guilty about it," said McQuarter,

grinning. "You've got a soft conscience. It's all over your face. What's the lady tellin' France this time?"

"I don't want no trouble with you," was Freckles uneasy rejoinder. "But, gosh, I dassen't tell that."

"Just between friends, you understand," explained McQuarter. Then, when the messenger seemed to lock his lips stubbornly McQuarter drawled a slow phrase that shook Freckles almost out of his skin. "What was you doin' a week ago in that little clump of pines north of France's range? I thought I heard a calf beller. None of my business, of course. Lots of boys make a little side money that way."

"Now listen—"

"I'm listen' to hear a message."

Freckles blurted it out all in a piece. "It says for France to meet Laurel in town tonight for somethin' real serious."

"Fine," said McQuarter and wheeled about. "You know what you know and I know what I know. It's our little secret. We'll keep it such. Bust along."

He rode furiously toward his ranch, increasingly enraged with every pace of the way. "She's warnin' him against me. She loves the man. Makes no difference how he feels toward her, she'll fight for him and throw herself away on him. That's Laurel. So he'll be in Crowheart tonight! Damn him, I'll break his neck!"

## CHAPTER VIII

The note from Laurel Annison, which reached John France directly after he had eaten the midday meal with Slim Hillis, was longer and contained more information than Freckles had divulged to Al McQuarter:

"John: I was coming over your way a little while ago with an invitation to try another of my meals. Perhaps I might be able to turn out chuck almost as good as Louise—and maybe that remark has a purring sound. But I met Al on the road and thought it wise to write this instead of coming. I am going to Crowheart this afternoon and will be there overnight—at the hotel. You must run in and let me tell you something. I wouldn't be asking you unless it was rather serious.—Laurel."

Slim Hillis, just ridden in from the east, watched the furrowing up of France's brow. "Bad news?"

"I can't make out," replied France. "But it sounds as if it might be."

"Useless question," grunted Slim. "All news comin' to us is bad. I wish I had six more men under my wing. I'd go ahead on suspicion and blast the hell out of Crowheart."

"Uh-huh," murmured France, tucking the note in his

pocket. "Are the boys finding any of our stuff?"

"Some—not enough. Plenty of old tracks on our range, though. Damn it, John, this business is under my collar. I'd venture to guess we're shy eight hundred to a thousand head of beef which has simply sunk into the ground. I'm likewise plenty certain that somewhere in these hills is a couple hundred head Circle IF stuff hidden this minute. But I've ridden myself poor in the flanks and ain't tumbled the spot yet. Some places a solitary man can't go in plain daylight. Which is why I wish for some more gents to back me up."

"All trails lead north, is that it?" said France.

"That's the way I figure," assented Hillis. "Eight hundred or more critters over the hump. Where to, I can't say. And we're too well watched to go and look.

"By the way, I had Canary Ellensburg drive those six loose horses down to the railroad under cover of dark last night, like you wanted. But what you aimin' to do with 'em?"

"That's the joker I've been holding in my hand for a spell, Slim. You put a leg up and amble across country, overtake Ellensburg before dark, and after the sun goes down drive straight for that culvert which is about twelve miles east of Crowheart. I'll follow you by a different route in an hour."

"Mystification," was Slim's good-humored mutter. "Well, if you got a hole card now's the time to slap it on the table. We been let alone as long as that gang ever lays off anybody. I feel a good swift kick in the makin'."

He strolled out and took to the saddle. He passed through the gate southward with a lazy melody in his throat and his hat skewed rakishly to one side of his head. A cool cucumber, this man Slim Hillis, with the head of a philosopher. A fatalist, a cheerful pessimist, he had long ago taught himself the only way of getting the ultimate squeeze of pleasure out of life—to take each day and hour as it came, asking no questions and anticipating almost nothing. Insofar as Slim was concerned, life was a series of troubles connected by deceptive lulls of peace. But if he knew the world would fall apart nine minutes away he would be apt to spend eight of them shaving, or curling a cigarette in the fresh sun. One thing at a time was his motto and the greatest concession to this mode of living he had ever made was to travel out of his serene path to help John France.

Meanwhile France was rocking himself in a porch chair and rereading Laurel Annison's letter, trying to fathom what lay between the lines. He had seen her yesterday up by Cottonwood Meadows and they had smiled away the embarrassment of the near quarrel, riding casually around the rim of the meadow. If there was trouble it had developed since then.

"McQuarter was headed up her way just a few hours ago," he mused. "Wonder if that's got anything to do with it? Or maybe the rustlers have finally started poaching on her range. No, she mentioned

McQuarter—and she wouldn't have done so unless she meant me to catch a warning from it. What the devil is he up to? The man's gone out of his way to offer me help. I don t just know how to take him. His talk rings as true as a fresh dollar but I judge he could be as cold and quick as a cat if he was minded that way."

He folded the note into a pocket and settled back in the chair. He would have to ride hard to cover the ground between the ranch, the railroad rendezvous and Crowheart in the space of an evening. More to the point, he was treading dangerous soil when he set foot in town. If he knew anything at all, he most certainly understood that the opposing forces had him marked for any kind of trouble they could inflict. Crowheart was a trap he had lately avoided; but nevertheless he would answer Laurel Annison's summoning.

He shifted the chair and studied the rising land northward. Yonder was the secret of his rustled stock. All trails led north and petered mysteriously out in the rugged, secretive terrain. In that direction concealment was easy while to the south any trail was open to the passing glance. Yet south was the direction of the railroad and the cattle market. By what process of juggling did the rustlers run beef into the isolated reaches of those hills and translate that beef into money?

"They can't absorb eight hundred head of stuff into their own brands. Not without leaving themselves open to exposure. They've got a market somewhere and it's up to me to find it. There is just one possibility. Tomorrow I think I'll take a ride and see if my hunch is right. If it is—"

A rider rose from the southern slope and drummed through the open gateway. Louise Drood reined before the porch, smiled brilliantly at him and stepped to the ground. With an impetuous gesture she drew another chair and sat down before him.

"How's everything, John? Glad to see me?"

"Always pleased to have company," replied France, somehow disturbed. "On your way to town?"

"Shucks, I'm not just company," retorted Louise with a pouting of lips. "How long is it going to take me to wear down that gentlemanly reserve? No, I m not going to town, though I told Pop I was. I just came over to see you. When I get a fit of nerves you're my best medicine. Compliment for you."

France nodded and held his peace. He felt the definite pull of a magnetic, almost primitive femininity. There was a reckless buoyancy about her that challenged his sober senses and made her presence both awkward and desirable; it was a part of her vivid personality. The flashing smile, the dark and expressive eyes, the rounding bosom—these things troubled him in a curious way, nor did it help any to know that the girl, with her appalling frankness, was unreservedly placing herself before him. He wanted to tell her that she was not wise in coming alone to this ranch but he could not find the words to fit. And as he looked the eager glow subsided from her eyes to be replaced by a haunting wistfulness.

"What are you thinking about, John?"

He studied the nearby trees a moment and finally plunged into the unpleasant expression. "Has it occurred to you this isn't wise?"

"Coming to see you? What of it? If I like you whose business is it but mine? I can't help being what I am. I don't care. I've got to find my own happiness. Nobody else will ever find it for me."

"Still," he persisted, "it isn't wise."

"What is being wise?" she asked, very softly. "To crowd things down inside yourself—to make yourself sad and lonely? Being here makes me happy, you don't know just how much. That is all the wisdom I ever want to have." Then another swift change came over the vivid, mobile features. The wistfulness darkened. She leaned forward, growing tense and her little white fists doubling up. "Oh, you're right—I know that! People can be so damn mean and small! I've got to tell you something. There's a story going around concerning us—"

France rose from the chair and swore under his breath. "I was afraid of that. I've helped you get yourself into trouble."

"You have not—this is my own affair! I've brought it on myself, and you. But if you can stand it I guess I can." She watched him with a tremendous intensity, saw the sudden firming up of his features and the pressure of his lips.

"It isn't right, my dear girl," he said quietly. "Since folks are made like they are it's no use your breaking your heart against public opinion."

She sat as still as a statue, hope and despair racing through her mind, pulled this way and that by a tempest of emotion. And then being Louise Drood, she played her last card. "Listen, John. I came over to tell you that my dad has got murder in his heart. He has heard the story. He has told the men of our outfit. He is meaning to catch you and lynch you. No—no, listen to me! I can stop that talk with just one word. You can't fight against the country when they believe that about you. They'll run you down. I can stop it by just raising my voice. But—look at me. What is my reward? Look at me, John France. Do you want me? What else do you want in a woman—what else could you desire? Don't you see? I could go in this house, close the door and never come out if you asked me to stay. Anything!"

She had risen, her compact body before him, her head thrown back that he might see the terrible earnestness, the complete surrender of her eyes. Standing there she was at that moment both beautiful and primitive—and tragic. The scene shook France and a sad compassion came over him as he reached out and with a finger brushed back one stray lock of her jet hair. And he spoke very gently.

"You'd better go home, Louise."

"Then," she cried, "I will not speak! I'll let them mob you! And when you are dying you'll think of me. I despise you!"

She stumbled down the steps and flung herself into

the saddle, racing away. Through the open gate she fled and around the turn of the ridge's lowering end. But of a sudden she whirled and came galloping back, crying like a broken-hearted child.

"Don't stay here alone tonight! They're coming then!" And she left him.

France rolled a cigarette somberly, cursing himself for the folly of ever allowing her on the premises. At first he considered it wholly his fault but presently a clearer vision tempered this conviction. Louise Drood was—Louise Drood. She lived at the end of her emotions, she was guided by the errant impulses of her heart. "I ought to have put my foot down on that business from the first minute," he thought. "The poor kid never had another woman to learn from, I guess. Now she's going to be followed by a dirty yarn. Somehow I've got to spike that. She deserves a better—she deserves a man she can spend herself on. I've got to help her."

It was time to be moving along. He went inside the house for a box of cartridges and his rifle. The rifle he slid into the saddle boot and the cartridges were distributed along his belt. Going out of the gate he closed it and took the Crowheart road south as the sun slanted half down the afternoon sky. At the split butte he left the town road and quartered easterly. Sunset found him in the rolling prairie around the Crazy Girl, and when dusk cloaked him with its blue tendrils of shadow he straightened out and hit directly for the rendezvous at the culvert.

As he traveled his mind kept veering from one girl to the other. Women were alike in many things, just as men were alike. The basic qualities of all the Lord's creatures were about the same. But otherwise a wide, unbreachable gulf lay between Louise Drood and Laurel. In the darkness he visualized Laurel's tall beauty and the strong, supple sureness of her manner. He had never ceased to marvel at the swift change she was able to make from the forthright bluntness of a business woman to the soft and graceful whimsy of the fireside. He doubted if he would ever fathom the contractions and the depths of her nature; doubted as well if he ever wanted to fathom them.

Sitting across from him that evening with her arms carelessly pillowed behind the glory of her auburn hair, Laurel had compelled his attention a hundred times more surely than the storm and fire of Louise Drood. Yet he never doubted for a moment that Laurel Annison had the same profound capacity for feeling that he knew Louise Drood possessed.

A faint glow wavered in front of him. A phrase of talk was sheered off and presently a soft command sifted through the shadows. "Sing out, brother."

"A friend," drawled France, "bringin' moral support."

He heard Slim Hillis chuckling. "Advance, friend. We'll accept the support but you needn't bother much about the moral business. Ellensburg and me has got it all doped."

"What's your mature conclusions?" asked France,

dropping to the ground.

"We figure you're aimin' to rob the east-bound just to keep your hand in shape. Now we have found a couple of loose ties down the track a ways which could easy be thrown over the rails to stop the choo-choo."

"I guess that's out," murmured France and heard the faint whistle of a train far off.

"Shucks," replied Hillis, "I was countin' on it. Never robbed a train myself and the experience would round out a comprehensive career in assorted misdemeanor."

"Like to try it, huh?"

"If you ordered the job done," stated Hillis, "we'd do it and no questions asked. By the way, Ellensburg almost ran into Drood's men on a private roundup by the big S in the Crazy Girl. But he crawfished back and wasn't seen."

"She's coming," said France, seeing the headlight of the engine growing like a white bomb. "Horses out of sight? We don't want publicity in this. All right. We'll shinny under that culvert."

"Modesty is a great virtue," complained Hillis, barking his head when he ducked under the culvert arch, "but it has drawbacks. You ain't thinkin' of pushin' the train off the track, are you?"

The rails began singing and light sheered out along the prairie. A short whistle broke through the night, whereat France grinned to himself. Then the train came rolling over the culvert with a slow clank of drivers, the hot hiss of steam jets and a squealing of

138

brake shoes. The last car rumbled past and stopped twenty feet removed. They heard boots strike the cinders one after another and muffled laughter that was challenged by a man's irate language. "Next time you pull a stunt like that on my train I'll make the bunch of you grayheaded!" And the eastbound rolled slowly away.

Boots crunched aimlessly around. "You plenty sure this was the place?" asked a voice. "It looks like a long ways from nowhere to me and I ain't in no shape to walk home."

"It's the place but I don't see nothin'," said another. France rose from the culvert and lifted his words toward the recent passengers. "Might see somethin' if you galoots would look around."

"Hey—that's the boy Jawn himself!" The group sidled from the tracks and came down beside the culvert. A muffled hilarity skirled across the peaceful earth. France closed in, struck a thumping blow against a man's chest and in return was very nearly knocked off his feet.

"How many of you came?" he wanted to know.

"You said six and six it is. But where's your pride? Hell of a note to ask a gent to fall off a train miles and miles from nowhere."

"How did you manage to do it?" pressed France. "I knew you'd work it all right but the details interest me."

The chuckles rose again and were hushed by one of the group. "You mentioned a culvert about twelve miles east of this here Crowheart. So when we passed the town we begin askin' the conductor about any such culvert. He told us, but he didn't see eye to eye on the proposition of lettin' us off. We had bought tickets to the next dump and by gum he meant we should get there, no less. Seems like it ain't proper to stop a train between stations. So—"

"So," broke in another, "we sat on his lap and hauled heavy on the air cord. She stopped."

"Brought your saddles, gear and guns?"

"Uh-huh."

France swung his arm toward Hillis and Ellensburg, though it was too dark for either man to be identified. "This fellow on my right is Ellensburg. Man on my left is Slim Hillis, foreman of the outfit. Slim, these boys worked with me up in Nevada and I know 'em like brothers. Too damn dark for introductions so we'll postpone that till daylight. Ellensburg, you better drive in the horses while I explain the situation."

"So," interposed one of the newcomers, "you went and bought you another mess of grief. Great stunt of yours."

"I wrote you the general lay of the land," France went on. "Didn't want any of you fellows riding into this mess unless you understood exactly the kind of a fight it is. Slim here rounded up five other boys that are plenty able to take care of anything within reason but we're still short of enough men to make a respectable showing. That's why I squalled for help.

140

Now we can count thirteen hands, including myself, and that's ample to stand up and spit back."

"You bet," said Hillis with a dry terseness.

"All right," added France. "Here's what I aim to do. Slim thinks we've got some hundred head of beef somewhere up in the pocket country, but we can't locate it. We also figure there's a leak out north of our place, but we can't locate that either. We're being watched pretty close and that ties our hands. Now, Slim, I want you to take these boys to the house, hand out grub for a couple day's cold snack, and then ride right into the rough country with them—tonight. Picket them at different spots, along the trail that leads over the hump, at the high points where they can see what goes on around them. One man at a place. Then come home.

"You fellows are to hide out where Slim puts you. Keep our eyes and ears open and let nobody see you. Nobody knows you're here and the rustling crowd, seeing Slim and the old crew hanging around home quarters, will figure the coast is clear. They'll move that stuff sooner or later and you'll see where it is and what they do with it. That's the layout."

"Napoleon himself," murmured Slim. "It's a neat scheme."

"When we find out, what then?" demanded one of the newcomers.

"Hit for quarters. We'll get organized and bust this rustling bunch to hell and gone!"

"I knew I'd like this vacation," said another. "Lead

on." Ellensburg came back with the horses and there was an interval of profane saddling up. Slim came back to France. "Ain't you ridin' back with us?"

"I've got to hit into Crowheart for a minute."

"That," was Slim's blunt reply, "is a fool caper. You got no business within forty rods of that town."

"I know, but I've got to go. You take care of the boys. We're all set for a showdown and I think we'll smash that gang within the next forty-eight hours. I'll be home by midnight."

"I wish I was sure of it," grumbled Slim and moved away. Presently the whole group rode off into the night. France waited till the drumming died away, then stepped into the saddle and followed the track toward Crowheart. Around ten o'clock of the evening he sighted the glimmering lights of the place, circled and came in from a blind quarter.

France was too old a head not to know the danger of this visit. He was picking a ginger path between the jaws of a set trap. Crowheart belonged body and breeches to the rustling faction. The honest men in the place didn't count—they formed no part in the official machine nor did they exert much influence upon it. Poco Finn wanted him in jail, and once he was in jail they would establish a case against him as the cold killer of Evernight and Golloway and a packed jury would put him out of the way. Nothing more certain than that.

France wondered how it was that Laurel didn't realize the danger of the town for him. Clearly she didn't or she wouldn't have asked him to come in.

Beside him was an old barn apparently abandoned. In front of him a hundred feet away ran the back end of the north building line. Occasional lights shone through windows and the kitchen door of the hotel stood wide open, showing a cook and flunkey moving within. At this hour conviviality had reached a loose and mellow peak around the saloons; a piano was tinkling off a flat melody and somebody in Ziegler's Resort bawled like a lonesome calf. But in this back area he found nobody stirring.

Leaving his horse within the shadowed protection of the barn wall, France walked forward. Two buildings to the right of the hotel, a yard-wide alley led through to the street. He advanced along this, hearing the click of pool balls and the rustling of shuffled cards through the thin walls. A window lifted a story above his head, and a whisky bottle was tossed out, missing him by inches. Then he stood in a dark niche of the street and looked either way.

Perhaps twenty men were in the street. Some were sitting out in front of the stable, others loitered on the courthouse steps. Scanning that group more closely, he wondered if Finn was there. A few citizens held down the hotel porch and as he studied this end of town he suddenly saw Laurel Annison's trim figure coming out of a drygoods store on the opposite side and cross over. Her cool, casual "Hello, boys," to the porch loungers reached France pleasantly.

Then, even as he threw aside one method of

approach after another, he made out the slightly unsteady Topeka Totten making a dignified departure from Ziegler's, just a few yards away. Topeka, France instantly decided, was a safe man or else Slim Hillis would not have befriended him. So he watched the shriveled alcoholic with a patient, anxious interest while the latter teetered in front of the saloon. The flip of luck went to France. Totten turned and approached the alley's mouth. When he was abreast of it France touched his arm, reassured him with a quiet word and drew him deeper into the darkness.

"France speaking, Topeka. You sober enough to know me?"

"Hell," protested Topeka, "I ain't drunk. Ain't even intoxicated. Listen. Shwift shea while the Miss—Mississ—' Well, anyhow I'm stone sober." Then the man caught hold of himself, straightened and grunted. "You here alone? Where's Slim? This ain't no place for you, Mr. France."

"I want you to do me a favor," murmured France. "Drift into the hotel and find out which room Laurel Annison's in. Don't attract any attention doing it."

"I'm gone," Totten said and departed. It seemed an extraordinarily long spell of waiting. Here and there lights began to die out of the windows and the street was thereby thrown into deeper gloom. The group on the courthouse steps dissolved. France watched the individuals of it closely as they split and ambled in different directions. A man walked in from the eastern street and intercepted one of those coming from the courthouse. After a short interval they both turned back. Then Topeka Totten sidled into the alley.

"Room ten, Mr. France. Which is on the second floor over in the northeast corner at the end of the hall. But you can't go through the front way 'thout being seen. Turn back. They's a kitchen door openin' into the rear of the hotel. This way from that kitchen door is another one that takes you up a flight of stairs. Say, are you sure nobody knows you're in town?"

"I don't think anybody's got wind of me yet," answered France. "Why?"

Topeka shifted his weight and grumbled. "Oh I dunno, but I've lived in this joint too long not to feel the shift of a breeze. I been thinkin' all evenin they was somethin' worryin' Finn and his friends."

"Thanks," France said and ran back down the alley. He pressed along the hotel wall till he located the designated door. Passing through the door he tip-toed up a black stairway and halted on the landing. A full glow rose from the lobby by the front stairs. Beside him a transom emitted a shaft of light and a sleepy conversation between a pair of drummers.

"So I says to Levy, 'I bet you a case of extra dry I can sell Schlossberg more goods outa my line in a day than you can in—'"

France crept back the upper hall to the last left-hand room and tapped softly on the panel. Laurel Annison's slow call invited him in. He opened the door and closed it quickly behind him, hearing someone coming up by the front stairs. Laurel had been writing at a desk. There was a furrow of thoughtfulness on her clear brow but when she saw France she rose quickly from the chair and crossed the room to pull down a window shade.

"John, I'm afraid I made a fool move. I didn't realize when I wrote that note—well, anyhow, I hadn't been in Crowheart a half-hour before I knew this was the last place you could safely be. Why didn't you disregard my note?"

She was in riding clothes and a jersey sweater fitted trimly around her sturdy shoulders. The lamp glow burnished her hair and deepened the grave, pensive beauty of her features. France took off his hat and settled in the extra chair. At once the tension of his situation and the weariness of the day's work fell away and was forgotten. "You said you wanted to see me," he said quietly. "And when you say that I'll go any place."

She flushed and her head rose to meet his glance more directly. "I believe you mean that."

"As I never meant anything else."

She looked down at her writing, pen point aimlessly tracing over the paper. Then she was smiling up to him, trying a little to hide her inner turbulence. "We are getting along better, aren't we?" Then the smile faded. "That makes it a little easier for me to tell you what I had in mind. I hope you don't feel—won't think that I'm trying to rope you into my troubles?"

"I'd certainly like to feel you were doing just that,"

he said. "It would make me think I was getting some-where."

"Do you doubt it?" she murmured and pressed her nether lip quickly between her teeth. The color of her cheeks deepened and then she hurried on. "A woman can do so many things that don't make rhyme or reason. Sometimes I marvel at man's patience and sometimes I—am afraid of man's lack of patience. Coming over your way this morning I met Al McQuarter on the road. It doesn't matter, does it, what we talked about? I won't tell you, not tonight at least. Some day I may. But I did tell him that whatever agreement we had gone on believing ever since we were beyond childhood had to be changed. Al is one of the finest men I know. That is all, John. Nothing more. If I've led him to believe otherwise for so long a time that's because I wasn't certain. I didn't know. I've always told him that, too. But this morning I had to clear things up, and Al took it badly."

He knew better than to break in. So he waited while she looked down at the table, frowning, disturbed, unsure of her words and trying to choose them care-fully. She went on, speaking faster and with more energy. "I've always known he had a temper but one of the things I liked most about him was his command of himself. It slipped this morning, John. Badly. Not so much in what he said, though he did speak to the point. But it was on his face. I've never seen him so cold and raging before. I'm afraid."

"Afraid of what?" asked France. "He's not the kind of

fellow to hurt a hair of your head. But if he tried—"

"It isn't that!" was Laurel's impatient interruption. "It's you—and him! The McQuarters have always been strong men, set like iron in their ways. They don't give up. They're not graceful losers. I never realized the terrible intensity of their temper until Al betrayed it today. John—he has the reputation of being faster and more deadly with a gun than any man who ever lived in this country!"

Silence clung to the room over the lengthening moments. France slowly revolved his hat between his fingers, seeming absorbed in the motion. A gradual deepening of lines appeared on his forehead; a settling and hardening of lip and chin. He raised his glance to the somber, worried girl. "I figured him for a fellow hard to beat in a way. Whatever else I may think about him I'll keep to myself, which is proper. I don't blame him for getting upset at losing out, Laurel. I'd like to talk to him straight from the shoulder and explain that, but it's just one of those things a man can't do. He'd think I was apologizing or maybe I was afraid. Or he even might figure I was rubbing in my brag. I'll have to leave him alone and let him make the first advance. As to gunplay, that's too bad. But if it's to be then it is just naturally to be and I'll hold up my end. Nothing else to be done."

"No! I won't stand for it. That's tragedy. Before I'll see you fighting I'll take the train out of Crowheart and never come back."

"Wouldn't change the situation a particle," he said

148

thoughtfully. "If it's in his mind and heart to brace me then nothing's going to sway him. Now you shouldn't be so troubled. It isn't a woman's fault if a man chooses to make a fool out of himself. Your mind is your own. You've got a right to change it any time. You've got the right to send him away, and me away. McQuarter's not playing according to rules. Even so, I guess I can't blame him too much. I might do the same thing. I believe in fighting to keep what I've won."

"You wouldn't," she broke in. "Not that way. You'd fight fair." She rose and came over to him. "I told you a woman could cause a man a world of trouble. Do you see it now? I've had to say things to you I never would have said under any other circumstances. Understand that, won't you? I had to tell you. Promise you'll keep watch for him, and that you'll not let him draw you into a fight."

He got up. "Does it mean a whole lot to you?" he said. "As far as I'm concerned?"

She met his eyes bravely, never halting. "Can you doubt it, after all that I've said?"

"Good Lord, Laurel—" His hat dropped to the floor and then she was fast in his arms, yielding without a sound, the sparkle of tears in the long look she gave him. And presently, after a stretch of silence that neither was aware of, he stepped back and reached for his hat.

"Then I'll promise nothing, my dear," he decided, huskiness in his voice. "I will not lift my hand to bring

149

on a fight with McQuarter. But I won't go out of my path to explain something he ought to realize without explanation. If he comes after me I'll not step aside. I've always had to fight for what came to me and nothing under heaven will ever keep me from fighting for you—except your own word that you don't want me."

"You'll never hear me say it," she whispered. "But I can't believe, I won't believe that you two—"

He shook his bead. "Men are proud fools, apt to do anything. Maybe that's the trouble with this world. Good night, Laurel."

He stepped quickly through the door, blinded by the darkness of the hall. When he reached the top of the back stairway he thought he heard the springing of a board near at hand. Placing his back to the wall he listened, but nothing more came to him but the fitful talk of the two drummers. Quietly descending, he opened the door into the back lots and started for his horse. At that instant a pair of crushing arms pinioned his own arms to his body, and a gun's muzzle pressed into his side with a cruel force.

"Stop right where you are, France."

That was Poco Finn's exultant, brutal voice. And Poco Finn's arm plucked his gun from the holster. "Now turn about and walk humble to the jug. By God, if we don't hang you as high as Monday's washin' I'll turn in my star and never arrest another man!"

There was no single chance for struggle or escape. He felt the presence of three men around him, and the gun never relaxed its pressure against his ribs. And so, with a strange caution, they forced him around the end of town and down to the back side of the jail. Ten minutes from the time he had left Laurel Annison he was behind the brick walls of the cell. All the suppressed hatred of the last few days of violence and lawless opposition rose up in John France to sear his veins with its furious power. Looking through the grating at Poco Finn, fingers gripping the bars until they were white, he said:

"Better for you if I am hung. Because if I'm not you will never be able to arrest another man."

Topeka Totten, whose life had descended from high places to low, lived on with nothing much but liquor and gossip to sustain him. Men spoke freely in front of him, regarding him as a harmless nonentity. As a consequence he knew almost every grimy detail in the life of Crowheart, and had seen more than anybody was aware of. He was as sensitive as a barometer, as sly as a savage. From force of habit he had slipped quietly to the back of town when France went into the hotel, knowing that Finn and Finn's man had been out for blood during the last few days. He was within ten feet of the capture. He could have touched France's elbow as the latter passed by in the grip of the three.

Turning like a rabbit, Topeka ran for the stable, in one dirty and remote corner of which was his home, his blanket, his useless trinkets. There also was the only valuable possession he had left—his gun. Except at train time he seldom wore it any more, for he was proud of his past and he knew that, being old and useless and shoddy, he only degraded the weapon with its smooth, worn handle. Yet tonight he strapped it around him and stepped to the street. A long while he stood there in the darkness, head lifting toward the black sky like an old dog vainly keening the breeze with blunted senses.

"All I got left," he murmured finally, "is the chance of dyin' like a gentleman—which I was onct. That lad is a man like the kind I rode with way back when the world was young. I got to lift my hand."

But first he had to have a drink. Into Ziegler's he tramped. He downed a stiff jolt of raw fire, wiped his lips and drank again—borrowing a fictitious manhood to supplement what little of his own remained. He loitered a moment, glooming over a past that extended back into an unreal remoteness, and a future that was surely and inevitably petering out in the shortness of these spring days. He waited for the glow and surge of power that drink provided, and when it came he squared his shrunken shoulders and walked quickly from the saloon. He had to have a horse and he meant to get one the easiest way.

At the eastern end of the street where the shadows were thickest he saw a horse standing up to a hitching rack. He walked to it, looked all about him and climbed stiffly into the saddle. Without discovery he got out of town and aimed northward for the Circle IF. He put the horse to a fast pace but after a little while, groaning with the misery of his disintegrating fiber, he had to draw in. But the pace was too slow. He would never get anywhere at such a rate. What little of sun and air he had left was best used in one headlong, reckless burst. Tonight he would spend it all at once. So, hardening himself to torture, he broke into a gallop again.

He didn't know that a rider sent out by Poco Finn preceded him on the trail by ten minutes.

## CHAPTER IX

In the absolute darkness of the cell, John France sat on the bunk edge, fought down the rage that was so fruitless, and began critically to examine his chances.

Normally a slow-moving man possessed of an easygoing, tolerant temper that got him through life very well, he found himself tonight looking at the world from the extreme opposite viewpoint. This was the culmination of a steady campaign on the part of the rustlers to destroy him and all that he owned. His enemies had used every weapon at their command. They had turned him into a gunman. They had made him kill—he who abhorred the taking of human life. They had even hurt the good name of a woman in order to rouse neutral opinion against him. And so now they had maneuvered and trapped him into helplessness.

Since they were bent on destruction, nothing would ever halt them short of their own ruin. It was his job to accomplish that ruin with neither mercy nor scrupulousness. In the darkness his slim fingers spread outward and he lifted his shoulders. "Hell of a time to be deciding that," he muttered. "They've got me squeezed down like a rat in a trap."

Nobody, he believed, had seen his capture. Nor would it have made any difference if someone had seen it. Outside of Laurel Annison, he doubted if there was a man in Crowheart able to help him. He had told Slim Hillis he would get home by morning. Slim would get worried by his nonappearance and backtrack, and he knew that the foreman was cagey enough to bring along as many of the crew as he could muster. Even so, he didn't see how that would help much. They couldn't break into the jail. Finn doubtless was guarding against just such a contingency—and probably hoping for it. By such an act he had a full and legal excuse for wiping out the Circle IF adherents.

It looked black enough. France rose, impatient at the blank alleys his thoughts kept running up, and went over to the window. The sash was raised and a cold night wind scoured through. A foot beyond and a yard below was freedom, made remote by the strong iron rods imbedded in the brick and cement work of the wall. Going back to the bunk he rolled a cigarette, smoked it to the end and relaxed on the blankets. "They've taken this trick," he mused, "but the game ain't finished yet. I'll sleep on it." And presently, throwing all reflections overboard with sound nerves and conscience, he was plunged in slumber.

It seemed to France that he had been sleeping only a moment when an abrupt, muttered command reached him. He opened his eyes to find a lantern flashing through the grating. A key turned the lock and Poco Finn was at the open door, ordering him out. Other men, he perceived, were lining the corridor and as he passed from the cell one of them thrust a gun against his back. "Hands behind you," the fellow growled, sullen and sleepy. "Hurry it up."

He had no time to obey. His hands were pulled roughly back. A slim rawhide thong noosed deep into his wrists and was tied. They shoved him ahead to the sheriff's office and halted a moment. During this delay he had a chance to look over his captors. There were five of them, excluding Finn—men he never had seen before, all bearing a manner of subdued yet harsh purpose. They stared at him with a strange and somber fixity and in a flash of thought France remembered such an expression on a man's face in the dim past, when that man was about to put the finishing bullet in a dog gone mad. An utter silence held the room. They scarcely moved, seeming to be waiting. France turned toward Finn.

"What seems to be on your mind?"

For some reason Finn answered without his usual rancor. "You can read signs, France. Look around. Your sentence is on the wall as clear as a fresh burned brand."

"So?" France said and all his muscles hardened. "A

lynching bee, is it?" His sudden, metallic laugh struck across the room. "And you turned the key that gave me away, Finn. You'll be apologizing to yourself the rest of your life!"

"Shut up that cacklin'!" said another of the group.

"Why be afraid of a little noise?" jeered France. "You remind me of a pack of yellow hounds cringing around a garbage can in the middle of the night. Its your town, ain't it?"

"Shut up!" cried the man with sibilant intensity, "or I'll smash your teeth in!"

"Brave boy," said France softly. "My hands are tied. Just naturally full of courage, ain't you? What makes you sleepy—you do most of your work at night, don't you?"

The man, for all his violent humor, flushed at the temples and stared strangely at France. "Tonight'll be the best night's work I ever helped do, mister. You can bet I ain't ashamed of it, either. Or afraid."

"Why should you be afraid?" retorted France. "I'm being lynched, not you."

Someone stepped into the office from the main hall. France swung about—to confront Crossjack Drood. In the yellow light this man's swarthy features were tainted with a peculiar yellow and his eyes burned with a fitful gleam in the recessed sockets. He seemed old and a little haggard. Something of the burly resilience was gone from his iron physique. Even so, France could see the dogged, malevolent purpose stamped on the rounding jaw.

"Your party, Drood?"

"Mine," Drood replied heavily, and threw the bitter, bludgeoning words over the room. "We run you down, finally. You've cut a wide swath through the country for one man. It's about time somebody taught you not to try to show your grandmother how to suck eggs. You lousy, low-crawlin' degenerate!"

"In other words, I'm interfering with your business of beef stealing."

"You know a whole lot, don't you?" Drood said. "That's part of it and I won't deny it. Why should I? But I tell you, France, the rope's not goin' around your neck for that. It's somethin' a damn sight worse, which you well realize. I never put up to be an angel myself, but I draw the line on one thing—and so does the rest of this country."

"Hell," France said, "you're just talking to make echoes. What's this so-called unspeakable crime? You're making a clumsy mess of covering up your tracks, Drood."

"Stand there and say you're ignorant!" cried Drood. "By God, I ought to use the knife on you first! That plain enough? No man can play loose with my daughter—"

"So?" murmured France. "Your daughter never told you that, Drood."

"Naturally she wouldn't. But I've heard."

Silence swirled heavily through the cold room. France shook his head. "I guess you really believe that, Drood, or you wouldn't be putting the mark of shame on her. I'll just say you're wrong. Your daughter is a fine woman, and you've got no credit coming for that, either, considering the example you've set her. She's better stuff than you'll ever be."

Drood flinched and at that moment he looked more haggard and worn than before. Then he set his jaws brutally and ducked his head at the other men. "Enough of this. It's time to be movin' out."

"Listen," broke in Finn, "you boys have got to keep me clear of this. Don't pull any rough stuff near town. I've got enough to do to produce an alibi as it is. Take him a long ways off."

"That's already settled," said Drood. "Outside with him."

France was ringed around by the party and moved down the courthouse corridor to the street. They boosted him up to a horse warm on the flanks from recent hard travel. A man closed to either side of him and his reins were taken by the rider ahead. And thus arranged the cavalcade went slow and silent through Crowheart, gained the open country and spurred northward on the well-worn trail.

France had thought it no later than midnight. But the eastern sky was paling and the sleeping prairie's outline began to roll under the thinning blanket of shadow. Day was not far below the line. As they traveled, urging onward at a straining pace, the sharp fog whipped against his clothes and into his body. Yet he was not cold as he would ordinarily have been. The ebb of fortune swept him out while the impulse of life, eager to go on living, sent warming waves through him. His thoughts were hard, clear and desperate. All his senses had sharpened, and he thought the smell of the damp grass and sage never before had been so pungently aromatic.

That was the irony of existence—these small things that all the years he had taken for granted now rose up to torture him with their preciousness. All this time his mind kept beating out to find some avenue of escape or survival, and found none. The party pressed against him. His hands were numb with the effort he had placed against the biting rawhide cord. It denied him even the opportunity of pitching himself off the horse.

Of a sudden—and it seemed they had covered the distance incredibly fast—the cone-shaped split butte was immediately in front of them. Thigh and thigh they passed down the defile, echoes rattling up and back the sides. At the far end Drood turned and led them around until the leveling west angle permitted them to rise toward the top. Halfway up he halted, and France saw a pine standing at his elbow.

"Taking me a long way to die, Drood," he said, hearing his own words come out flat and brittle.

"This is where you killed Golloway," was Drood's taut answer.

"Revenge with plenty of English on it," muttered France. "You sure have thought of everything. Dug a grave yet?"

"That's for the buzzards to do." Then Drood was standing in his stirrups and calling around the rock-strewn slope. "Where's that fool Limpy? I left him around here to keep his eyes open. Limpy!"

"It's gettin' light," grumbled one of the party. "We better haze this business through and cut along.

"Damn Limpy! He'd ought to been down there on the trail where I stationed him. All right, I guess he got scared of his shadow. Toss a rope over that left hand branch. France, it's so long for you. There's a good hot spot in hell waitin' and I wish to God I could sit in a while to see you burn!"

"I wouldn't worry about that," France droned, and wondered why his nerves should seem to freeze and leave him so strangely stolid. Life was mighty fine and the best of it had been before him. Laurel Annison. . . . He shook his head and remembered a long lost phrase of his father's. No man had fulfilled himself until he had died like a gentleman. It didn't seem as hard to do as he had figured. "I wouldn't worry about that," he repeated. "You'll be there by and by. You damn poor fools! You're signing your own warrants, every last man of you. The hills are full of my friends at this minute, and they'll never pull the saddle until you're accounted for."

"Throw the rope over," snapped Drood.

"And I'll repeat, not for your benefit, but for your daughter's good name, that she is a thousand times straighter than you ever thought of being. Now, blast your yellow hides, throw the rope over and get it done with!"

The first streak of day cracked the eastern horizon.

A rider sent his rope up into the tree and then a slow, competent voice rose out of the very earth nearby.

"That's about enough of that horse opera! Let me hear them elbow joints pop or we'll blast the bunch of you clean off this butte!"

Something inside John France, pressed down to bursting broke like a bomb. He capsized from his saddle at a single plunging move and struck the ground as a blast of gunfire set his horse to plunging. An iron hoof missed his head by the degree of a feather. Drood's answering burst of passion sailed over the slope. The fusillade thickened and a rider of the Drood string pitched out and down beside France.

France heard Slim Hillis sing out a warning to be careful where the bullets went, and a second yell to rise and attack. Drood bellowed again but the men behind him broke ground and fell along the slope a dozen yards, to make one more stand. One of that outfit was deliberately drawing a bead on France, who felt the lead strike around him. The Circle IF bunch had broken from shelter. He heard them racing in toward him and then a last furious series of crackling detonations died into a headlong rattle of hoofs down the rocky butte side. France rolled over and saw Slim Hillis running madly toward him.

"John! Hey, John—they didn't plug you? Sing out, man! By God—"

"Hang onto your pants," said France. "I'm trying to pick out the star I had a ticket for a minute back."

"Jumpin' Jasper," Hillis said. "Don't ever do that

161

again! I thought sure as thunder they'd busted up your plumbin'. Ellensburg, hoist back after the ponies. We got no time to lose on them—" and the rest of it sputtered like firecrackers going off in a string.

"Here," interrupted France. "Come cut this thong. I'm about paralyzed. How long you been behind them rocks?"

"A half-hour," Hillis said, reaching for his knife.

"You certainly did let 'em carry the program to the last inch," said France. "Must of interested you to see a hanging. How in hell did you know they were coming here, anyhow'?"

"Topeka Totten seen you arrested and hauled out of Crowheart for our place. The boys was sleepin' and I'd just got back from postin' your new men. We saddles and skins for town like a dog with a wet itch. Topeka was worried. He's got ears that lop over the whole county, and he figured they'd make this kind of a play. When we got to the butte here and started through we slammed right into one of Drood's riders. Busted right into him a-saddle. That got us all het up and suspicious of somethin'. So we pumped him— usin' some primin' material to make him talk. He squawled plenty—you bet he did. Drood had left him back to watch the butte while the main bunch come into town, got you, and returned here. I dunno why all the ceremony, but that sure was the story, so we clumb up here and waited. But, man, maybe you think we didn't sweat buckets of blood wonderin' if maybe Drood would change his mind on the location."

"I can sympathize with your harrowed emotions," drawled France. "Yeah, I can dimly understand 'em." He rose, pounding his hands against his chest to bring back feeling. "Now the next—"

One of the men cried out from the line of rocks behind them. "Here—fellows, look over here!"

Hillis started and flashed a sharp glance around the group. Then he muttered "Topeka," and broke into a run. France followed, stepped over the rocks and found Slim kneeling on the ground beside the shriveled body of Topeka Totten. The old man was lying with his face to the breaking day, a bullet's bluish gape in the center of his forehead. He was dead, yet about him was a look that might have been resignation or the knowledge of peace to come. Whatever the last thought, it was not fear or regret.

Hillis looked up with a strained face, saying nothing. Then he got to his feet and stared over the rim of the butte to the north where the fleeing Drood party were on the point of disappearing into the convolutions of the hills. Ellensburg cantered across the butte top at that moment with the horses and Hillis shifted toward France, mutely asking for a decision.

France shook his head. "No hurry about following them this minute. We'll take Topeka to the ranchhouse first and get fresh horses. I'm sorry, Slim. The old man played his last chip for me and I'm not forgetting. I want him to sleep back of the house where Ike is—and where I'll be some day. Then," said France and drew in a long breath, "we'll take out to wind up this busi-

163

ness. I'll never stop now till that gang is smashed to dust and ruin."

He swung on his heel, leaving Slim alone for the moment. The Drood rider who had fallen in the scrap was dead and scowling at the world so summarily and violently left. France took the man's gun, sighing as if he were tired, lips straightening to a single thin line. Then he got into the saddle of the same horse on which they had led him out of Crowheart, and reined around. The rest of the group were stringing through the rocks, Slim Hillis bringing up the rear with Topeka Totten's wire-drawn body cradled in his arms. An hour later they were at Circle IF and Topeka was lying on his last bed.

The Chinaman had breakfast in his oven and at sight of the returning crew he threw it on the table. But not until they had turned their horses into the corral and roped out fresh ones did they return to eat. Even so, the food might have been tasteless for all the thought these grimly silent men gave it. Not a word passed across the table. They were locked in sullen thought, possessed by a savage impatience to be away and doing. France, drinking his coffee, studied them closely and he realized then how well Slim Hillis had chosen.

There was nothing striking or flamboyant about these fellows. They were humble workaday riders with the dust of prosaic labor hanging to their clothes. They would have passed unnoticed in any crowd. Yet he saw the hardness of their jaws and the glint of their eyes, aflame with smoldering anger and he knew that wherever he rode they would be close behind. For a moment he was heavy-hearted with the thought of what the day meant. He was sick of fighting, weary of intrigue and struggle. But there was no choice. What the corrupted law of Crowheart would not do he had to do. So he rose, never touching his plate, and went to the porch.

Almost immediately they followed him, still wordless, waiting his command to go. He went around to the saddle boot and drew out his rifle, worked the breech, and slid it back to place. He looked to the fresh sky and the sun rising clear and hot from the east. Then he turned to them, on the point of speaking. But before he said anything a rider came catapulting down from the north trail and flung his pony to the porch. It was Elba Niles, one of the hands France had called from Nevada. Elba never stepped to the ground.

"All right, John, we got sight of them birds finally. Dewey McGinn heard brutes movin' over a ridge into the main trail before light and come back to tell me. We followed until day come. About three hundred head goin' straight north to the open country beyond. They're drivin' easy and not much hurried. Right along the open road. Eight men in the bunch, which I don't understand why they need so many for a two-man job. They'll be six—seven miles from here now. I skun back, leavin' Dewey in the brush to keep track."

France absorbed the information and turned it over

in his mind. "They timed it well. Figured to get the beef out on the road while I was in trouble and the rest of the ranch slept. That sounds like Drood's work. He must've split his crew, half to take care of the cattle and half to take care of me."

"Maybe," Hillis said. "Also maybe they's other outfits on deck."

France turned to his foreman. "Gonoway's men?"

"And maybe still others," added Hillis.

France's eyes narrowed. "I never gave any other outfit—meaning just one other in particular—much serious attention, Slim. If you thought so why didn't you say something earlier in the game?"

"Only a suspicion, John. I ain't tarrin' up anybody with guesswork. I aimed to find out first."

"Well, we'll let Drood personally alone for the time being. First we'll come down on the bunch fogging our cattle. I want all the boys in from the hills. You're the only one who knows where to find them, Slim. You strike out, draw them into the main trail and wait for me. I'll give you a half-hour's start."

"All I need," said Slim and threw himself into the saddle and was off.

France turned to Elba Niles. "Go get something to eat. Ellensburg, rope out a fresh horse for Elba. We've got plenty of riding ahead. No—wait a minute! Some bunch coming from Cottonwood trail. Spread out and stand fast."

A group of five or six men came single file through the trees, crossed the creek and collected to a more reassuring pace. France saw the freckled Annison rider foremost, and Freckles, observing the taut attention of Circle IF, suddenly threw up a hand. "All right, France, don't you know friends yet?"

"Come ahead," called France. "This is our nervous morning."

The Annison men turned in to the porch and the situation relaxed with a passing of talk between outfits. Freckles nodded his head at France. "We want to throw in. That all right?"

"What do you know about this business?" challenged France.

"The birds and the bees and the tall flowers noddin' on their stems have got a way of saying things," responded Freckles with casual irony. "We ain't blind, we ain't deaf. We'll apologize right off for hornin' into your affairs, but seeing as this is a wide open scrap we'd like to join it. You ain't thinkin' to turn us down?"

"What's Laurel—Miss Annison got to say about it?" asked France. He wasn't sure what he ought to say. The last thing he wanted was to draw her into trouble.

"She went to Crowheart yesterday afternoon," drawled Freckles. "Said she wouldn't start back till the noon mail come in." Freckles tried to keep a guilty knowledge out of his eyes and failed, so he ended by grinning shrewdly at France. "What difference does that make? We're a straight outfit and she'd be the last to complain. I guess maybe you know somethin' about that."

"I can use the help," agreed France, "and if you fellows want to borrow trouble I guess it's your business. But get it straight—I'm running the show and I want my orders followed. No turning off for your own private picnic."

"Agreeable to it," was Freckle's laconic reply.

"Light and eat, then."

"No thanks, we've et."

France looked at his watch, waited five minutes and rose to his horse. Instantly the group formed behind and followed him out of the yard and straight up the north trail. It paralleled the creek a quarter mile, stumbled into rugged ground and began weaving left and right to take advantage of the gradual grades. A mile on and five hundred feet higher the trail suddenly straightened to a stiff climb while the ridges closed in to make a deep defile. France called back of him. "Ellensburg, you go ahead of us a quarter mile and scout the trail. And I want a man to angle up each of these ridges and flank us."

He slacked off a little while to give them a chance to get ahead, then resumed the full pace. The trail, still climbing, began to delve into deeper timber, the ridges frowned down and the sun was cut off. Ellensburg had disappeared, but when they galloped around a knee of the left ridge they saw him stopped in front of Slim Hillis and the recalled pickets. The parties joined. Hillis stared at the Annison contingent and could not suppress a slight jeer. "What's this, a family reunion? We've had to work for our fun and now we got to cut

168

the cake with a lot of visitors."

"They'll be plenty of cake, don't you worry none," retorted Freckles.

"Keep going," said France.

A mile farther they cut the wide, fresh trail of cattle coming down the slope of the left hand ridge and heading north. France never stopped, but Hillis drew abreast to talk. "They come from Drood soil, you bet. He's been nursin' 'em yonder in some black hole that old Nick himself couldn't locate."

"We'll pay him a visit soon enough," said France quietly, and he thought of Louise Drood with the sad wistfulness lying in her eyes. A black country, a black house and a black father—that was all she had ever known. He shook his head, clearing out the thoughts. No time now for woolgathering. The trail began to warn him. They were near the end of the long upward climb and he could see the sky ahead hovering over open land. The ridges were pulling away, about ready to sprawl and dwindle into the northern flatness. Ellensburg, crawling on his stomach in advance, reached the summit, looked a moment and turned to fling up his arm. France led the party to within twenty yards of Ellensburg, then signaled for a halt. He got down and went forward with Hillis. Side by side, the three of them hitched across fifty feet of flat surface and then stopped. Below them was the herd.

The intervening distance was between a quarter and a half-mile down a long, abrupt pitch of trail that opened into a grassy bowl. The ridges spread out like the splaying of two fingers, the trees dwindled, and on ahead were the fresh, unmarked miles of plain stretching into the horizon. The bowl marked the end of the hills. At this juncture lay the herd, drawn to a halt, while the rustlers moved idly about and a few men, afoot, seemed to be holding a parley.

"Eight men, my eye," growled Hillis, "I'm countin' twenty and I think there's more."

"I wonder if Drood joined in to warn them?" mused France.

"Wouldn't be surprised," replied Hillis. "But all told he ain't got more'n twelve thieves in his outfit. Mebbe four-five of the old Golloway outfit has thrown in with him. That means there's still another set of rascals in the party. Now I'm wonderin' who?"

"Soon find out," murmured France. He absorbed the scene at a long, thoughtful glance. His face pinched in. "We're going down there."

"It'll be a pitched fight, don't figure any less," said Hillis, carefully casual.

"Then let it be so. Come on back."

He drew the party around him, rolled a smoke and studied the grave faces that looked to him for leadership. "Slim figures it will be a pitched fight," he said slowly. "And I think he's right. They're too far in the red to give up humble. Also, they outnumber us by two or three guns. But we're goin' down. Any objections on that?"

"Ask the tourists that question," said Hillis with a dusty-dry grin, indicating the Annison outfit.

"Shut up!" snapped Freckles. "We'll show you the way down that hill."

"No, this isn't going to be any cavalry charge," broke in France. "That's the sucker's way of doing it. We'll angle to the left and get on the blind side of the ridge. You Annison fellows stop about a quarter-mile along it. The rest of us circle around the low point and ride in from the far end. That puts us all pretty close before they get time to organize hostilities. I don't aim to go in shooting. We ride in easy and tell them to take their choice. Then it's up to them. Jail or war. When you Annison boys hear the first shot, break over the ridge and bust down into their flank."

"Is there a parson in the group?" murmured Hillis, eyes half shut.

"You tryin' to make me nervous?" challenged Freckles.

"Not for the world, my son. I love you, paint face and all. But I sure suggest you Annison lads write your true names on a piece of paper and tuck 'em in your pockets."

"Tell that to your own collection of jail birds," snorted Freckles.

"You always was such a moral outfit," drawled Hillis. "That's why I never worked with you." Then he sobered and fell silent.

All eyes swung to France. He got to the saddle, seemed to lose himself in thought a long moment, and then murmured, "Here we go."

They swung well to the left, put a small shoulder of

the ridge between them and the rustling party, gained the thinning trees and fell behind the opposite face of the spur. All along the chase there had been some exchange of talk. Now nobody spoke, not even when the Annison group broke clear at France's gesture and halted. The lowering spur brought them nearer the rustling party and they heard a cow bawling in the bowl. Presently they were veering to the right with the last of the trees behind them and only a fragment of rolling contour concealing them. France reined in, chose his location and pushed straight across the spur. The rustlers appeared before them, fifty yards away.

So far France's men had kept bunched. Now he felt them swing out in a fanwise arrangement. Hillis was to his immediate left, and an old friend of his Nevada days, Dewey McGinn, rode to his right. It was strange, but for a space in which he could have counted ten no sound of warning rose from the rustlers, no yell of discovery. Then a wild, rocketing shout soared from one man at the far end of the herd and the whole gang whipped into motion. France's eyes were at the moment pinned on the men dismounted. He recognized Drood's black head as it bobbed up in startled astonishment and another he knew to be one of the original Circle IF crew he had fought off the ranch. The others—three of them—he didn't know.

All this while the rustlers were flinging their ponies forward, closing the gap. He heard Hillis saying, in a tone that seemed disappointed, "I don't see a damn soul from Al McQuarter's!" Dewey McGinn yelled like a Comanche and poured steel into his horse as a straggling fire broke from the rustlers. There would never be a chance to offer those lawless marauders their choice. They had chosen instantly; they would fight. The drag end of France's party, flanked by Ellensburg, came snapping around and so the opposing factions plunged ahead for the bitter impact. France lifted his gun and spurred the horse beneath him with a rising, fiery fury.

He wanted to reach Drood, but the man was off at the right end of the attacking line, and France could not quarter across the line of fire. From the corner of his eye he saw Drood stumble back, fall to a knee and open up, then fling himself behind the protection of his nearby horse. Then something peculiar happened. The three fellows he hadn't recognized threw up their arms almost in unison and stepped out of the arc of plunging lead. They never made a move to draw. They were surrendering.

All this he saw in a flash as he was drawn into a mad whirlpool of passionate destruction. The smash of revolver play was like nothing he had ever heard before in its swift, deafening reverberations. The interval closed up before any of them were aware. A shock rended the parties, saddles emptied, horses went staggering down and a high scream sheered above the coarser brutality of gun echoes. Then all order and sense of direction was lost in the twisting, smoke-tainted confusion. It was man to man, a vicious melee with animal and human jamming together, struggling clear and smashing in again.

A hard, cold core of reason kept France's mind clear, but he saw all this through a red film that he couldn't shake away, and there was a strange warmth creeping down one cheek. Powder belched in his face. He was battered by an explosion and a horse's front feet lifted and towered above him, about to sweep down and knock him senseless. He swerved and caught the rider against the sky. The man faded from his vision.

France plunged onward, was side-swiped by another of the gang turning to meet the attack of Slim Hillis. France stood in his stirrups and laid the barrel of his gun across the rustler's head, wilting the renegade with the blow. Slim's wiry cheeks, pale with excitement, broke into a wrinkled grimace that was meant for a smile. "Experience sure makes a well rounded man!" he shouted across the narrow space. He veered, ducked and vanished.

The whole embattled mass shook with some vaulting shock and France lifted his eyes to see the Annison riders fling themselves into the melee. That battering was enough to shake the earth. Suddenly the pressure of resistance loosened. The renegades were fighting away. But as they did so, the herd, milling fretfully, broke into full stride and stampeded across the bowl toward the eastern ridge.

The edge of the herd caught men and horses and flung them apart like straw stems. France found himself fighting his way out of a bawling pandemonium. Never trying to run against the pressure, he raced with the momentum and edged clear. A black-haired, black-faced figure shot into the lee, saw him and hauled around with a desperate, savage haste. It was Drood. The man's gun came around in one impetuous move. France saw it and though the fighting urge was like fire in his veins, one lonely impulse streamed through his nerves and made him elect to chance it out. They were but two scant yards apart, side and side. France's gun spoke first. Drood's arm flopped back, his weapon dropped and the fresh blood ran free on his finger tips.

The stampede had carried both parties up the side of the ridge. The cattle were laboring over the crest, the men turning back, and as France took in the whole situation, he saw a pair of hands shoot into the air in token of surrender.

At that France raised his voice to the level limit of his power and cried out, "Pitch up! You've had your medicine! Pitch up and make a stand or you'll never see another day!"

Even as he said it the centaur-figured Ellensburg raced far around the group, towing half a dozen others, crimping in the rustlers, cutting them off from flight. So whipsawed, outnumbered now, and outfought, they caved in. A final shot sounded strangely flat and futile in the air, and hands lifted. It was over.

"Sit solid where you are!" warned France. "Close in, boys. Strip 'em clean. Bunch 'em together."

He swung back. Drood was sitting cross-legged on the ground, hauling a bandanna tight around his bloody wrist with teeth and free arm. France drew in and looked down. "Got a bellyful of this, Drood?"

Drood's murky eyes raised and dropped. He had nothing to say. France spurred his horse on back to where the three strangers had stood aloof from the very beginning. It had not seemed possible that so much ground had been covered, yet the distance from their location to the surrendered rustlers was almost the whole length of the bowl. The strangers saw him come and lifted their arms again. He whirled before them, dropped down and whipped out their guns.

"Listen," said one of them, almost as fat as Lawyer Kidder, "this ain't our quarrel. You got us wrong."

"That so?" snapped France. "A man's judged by the company he keeps around here. What's your outfit? What brought you here?"

"My name's McGarrity," said the fat fellow, sweat rolling down his face. "I'm commissary purchasin' agent for the construction outfit buildin' the railroad north of here. What am I doin'? I'm buying beef from these gents, or was when you let hell out of the handbag. I had a call to come and look over a bunch of steers. So I come with a couple of my men. I'll ask your leave to pull out of this mess."

Before McGarrity had finished talking, the last mystery of the ring stood revealed. This was where Circle IF beef had gone.

"Hold on," France said. "You're in no hurry. How much beef have you been buying from these fellows?"

"Oh, considerable," confessed McGarrity, vague

and cagey. "Couldn't say offhand."

"You'll have time to recollect," snapped France. "How long has this been going on?"

"About six months. Now see here—"

"Do you understand you've been buying rustled stock?"

"I buy beef," replied McGarrity, trying to collect his anger. "I pay for it. That's all I got to do with it."

"Who gets the money?" pressed France.

McGarrity paused and seemed to take stock of his situation. "Do I get clear if I tell?"

"I'm not bargaining with any such cheap John grafter as I can see you are," was France's even statement. "But don't try to hedge on me. Do you see what we've done to that outfit? There's still a spoonful of medicine in the bottle. Who gets the money?"

"He ain't here," grumbled McGarrity. "Was to've been but he never come."

"Say the name," France told him, "or I'll sweat the lard off your back."

"McQuarter!" the fellow half-shouted.

France drew a great breath. "My God, when will I ever get to the end of this affair? Catch up your horses and fall in with that party. I'm sorry to say you're no better than they are. You're worse. You play both ends of the game—help steal from me and rob your own company at a fancy figure. You're going to jail."

"You can't do that!"

"Don't tell me what I can't do." France's eyes emitted a slicing, gleaming light. He swung a hand toward the field. "Look over there. One of my men died in this scrap. Those other three lying on the sod are your friends—paid off in full for rustling. Maybe you haven't got it through your thick head yet what this is all about. We came down here to do a chore, and we've done it. Such law as there is in Crowheart today you see right here. It's a poor time to talk about your rights with the smell of blood in the air. Now get over yonder."

He hazed the trio across into the group of herded rustlers and issued his blunt instructions. "Keep these fellows cool. They represent the big business angle in this game." Then he swung back.

Ellensburg and Slim Hillis were bending over the figure of a man—over all that remained of Mexico Sperry. Slim rose and turned toward France with a peculiar tensity of features.

"I'm sorry," said France, with a gruff bluntness. "All this was in the books before you and I were born. Can't change what was meant to be. Ellensburg, I'm leaving you behind to watch things here. I'll send a man back with a team and wagon from Circle IF. Let's go, Slim." He rode past the grouped outlaws and nodded his head. The whole cavalcade moved onward. In going by he saw Drood sitting dazed and bareheaded in the fresh sunlight, sunk in his own thoughts of disaster. The man looked at him and through him.

Slim galloped abreast and settled into a long silence. After a while France saw him shake himself and rouse. "France," Slim said, "you're a harder specimen than I figured."

"Easier to keep moving ahead than to think," was the tall man's sober comment.

"Gospel truth. I reckon I must be softenin' up under punishment." A dry mirthless laugh came out of Slim Hillis. "I was thinkin' about Mexico Sperry. Five minutes ago he was a drinkin', swearin' fool that never drew a peaceful breath. Considerin' his dislike of law and sheriffs and the constituted order of things he'd sure be the first one to laugh when he looks down and sees folks make a hero out of him over this day's work. I rode many a year with Mexico. Hell!"

"You were right about McQuarter," said France and repeated McGarrity's recent confession. Slim's blue eyes began to flicker and he motioned over the west ridge. "It's six miles to McQuarter's ranch. And they won't be any better time to knock him out of the tree."

"I considered it," agreed France. "But we haven't got the men to spare now. Our next business is to take this bunch into Crowheart and jail 'em. Then clean up the town, find Poco Finn and throw him in his own cooler. We never leave Crowheart out of our possession until the judge pronounces sentence."

"Meanwhile McQuarter's on his way to parts unknown," objected Slim. "But I ain't tryin' to run your business."

"McQuarter," replied France, quietly, "will never leave the country before he tries his luck with me personally. He won't run until then. I'm banking on that,

Slim. I'm looking forward to it, as sure as the sun goes down."

They were a mile on before Slim Hillis spoke again. "If it comes," he muttered, "the sun will go down for one of you."

"What is to be, is to be. Let it go at that."

They came to the ranch in the middle of the morning, and halted. France detailed Big Jones to go back to the bowl with a team and wagon. "Mexico Sperry," he said, "is to stay on the place and be buried here. As for the others, bring them on in to Crowheart. The town has got to see what happens at the end of the crooked trail." Freckles had to drop out with a bad leg and one of his Nevada friends likewise withdrew from the party, nursing a flesh wound in the shoulder. France pointed ahead again and they rode on through the gate, into the prairie and through the defile of the split butte. Near noon they entered Crowheart.

At the very edge of town France suddenly woke out of his somber study, picked Slim and four others, and galloped ahead. "We've got to catch Poco Finn before he gets the chance of setting himself. Two of you fellows edge into Ziegler's and look around for him. Come on, Slim."

The advance of the party filled the street instantly. A man came to the hotel porch, took one short look and dived back. There was a commotion in the livery stable and a citizen started out a-saddle. Hillis barked at him. "Get off and rest, you! Don't be in no hurry to leave."

France sprang down to the courthouse steps and started in. At the door he drew up. Poco Finn was coming out, curiosity on his face. When he saw France he stopped in his tracks and swayed, features sagging with the shock of astonishment. France never knew whether the man had courage enough to draw or not, because that pause was Poco Finn's undoing. France's gun was against him, and soundlessly, Finn lifted his arms and permitted himself to be stripped of his weapon.

"Where's the cell key, Poco?"

Poco's slow mind grappled hopelessly with the unexpected. Words jammed inside him. In a deadlock of uncertainty and defeat, he just stood there. France patted the man's coat and found the keys.

"You see the game's over, don't you, Poco?" he inquired gently.

Poco's eyes followed down to the gun and back to France's face. "I thought you was dead."

"You remember what I told you, Poco. I said that if I wasn't killed it would be the end of you. And it is, though I don't find the necessity or inclination of doing to you what I promised myself I'd do. Turn about and march to the cell."

The rustlers came stolidly in, driven like cattle. They turned through the sheriff's office and down the darker hall to the cell. France opened the iron door and tallied them through, then locked it and gave the key to Hillis. "You're sheriff, pro-tem, Slim. One of you fellows go hunt up the doctor. Drood needs attention and so do some of the others." Back in the hall, he set four of his men aside. "Don't leave the building. Let nobody come or go."

Slim came out of the sheriff's office, frowning. What next?"

"I want you to take as much help as you need and rustle through Crowheart. If you see anybody you think might make trouble for us or try to organize a rescue, throw 'em in."

"That's kind of high-handed, ain't it?" inquired a voice from an adjoining doorway.

France turned to see an elderly gentleman with mutton-chop whiskers and a frock coat.

"Gentlemen," said Hillis, "we have with us His Honor the Mayor."

"It is high-handed," returned France bluntly. "But I'll take the responsibility for that. My word goes until we get something that resembles straight law in here. Slim, if he kicks about it, throw him in too."

He went out of the courthouse, and Slim's voice stopped him. The foreman's wiry face was puzzled. "Listen, we sort of got the bull by the tail, ain't we? You got 'em jailed all right, and you got Crowheart just where you want it. But what next? I don't trust no judge around here."

"I'm about to fix that now," said France. "You go ahead. And don't be too gentle."

He walked swiftly down the street and around to the railroad station, catching the attention of the station agent.

"Give me a blank for telegraphing," he said. "No, never mind that. Just send this message along to the governor of the State: Sir, After a week's lawlessness, an attempted lynching, two pitched battles and the death of five men, I respectfully beg to state that we have taken the law into our own hands and arrested the sheriff and a score of persons openly caught at rustling and selling cattle. My urgent request is that you send a special representative, prosecutor and officers down here to take charge. Until that time Crowheart has nothing more than vigilante rule." He paused. "I guess that does it. Sign it my name. You know what my name is, don't you?"

"Damn well right," said the agent. "I'll push it over the wire now."

France re-crossed the street, aiming for the hotel. But when he saw Lawyer Kidder hurrying out of his office stairs, he swung and intercepted the man. Kidder came to an uncertain stand, his little eyes darting across France's face.

France drove right to the point. "Kidder, I have nothing I can hang on you. You're too wise. But there isn't the shadow of a doubt in my mind that you're head over heels with this gang."

"You bet you ain't got nothin' on me," snapped Kidder. "Nor never will."

"Don't be proud of it," was France's sharp reply. "I am giving you one hour to shake the dust of Crowheart."

Kidder began to protest. France cut him short by

turning away. Ten feet off he heard Kidder crying. "You won't be here in an hour to carry out that bet, France! I'll see you dead in the street before I go to supper tonight!"

France threw up his head, suddenly aware that the citizens of Crowheart were backing away from the exposed part of the street. He saw them withdraw to alley apertures, into the stable. It was as if some brazen gong of warning had clanged through the hot midday air—so abruptly did Crowheart tighten up to a watchful, guarded expectancy. France angled across the street for Ziegler's, feeling the weight of all this falling upon him, gray eyes narrowing against the sunlight and sweeping the shaded corners for treachery.

Louise Drood came running out of the courthouse and ran past him, casting a frightened, half-defiant glance at him and going on to the hotel without opening her mouth. Where she had been a quarter-hour earlier France didn't know, but here she was—a part of this scene of impending violence.

He heard his name called. Swinging, he saw Louise hurrying into the hotel and Laurel Annison coming quickly down the porch steps. He came over to her, observing the tremendous gravity of her eyes. Her face was white and drawn.

"John—I just heard all about this a minute ago! I never knew—come into the hotel for a little while. I want to talk to you."

She was trying to draw him away, to shield him against what lay ahead. The threat of it was singing through Crowheart, striking every last soul. France smiled at her. "Not now, Laurel. In another quarter-hour I'll come. Have you eaten? Well, then, I'd be pleased if you'd wait and eat with me. It's my treat, isn't it?"

Her voice sank to a hurried whisper. "Al's in town." The smile left France. "I thought it must be something like that. All roads lead to Crowheart today."

France paused and then went on, seeming sleepy. "Laurel, if it's in your heart I wish you'd go up and talk a minute with Louise Drood. It's been tough on her all around and a woman's comfort might help her some. They've tried to smut up her name. I've broken up her home and half-killed her dad. You go up."

"What about yourself, John?"

"That will develop pretty soon," he said.

"And what about me?" she asked, her voice sinking.

"I will ask you to answer that—when I come back. You had better go inside now, Laurel."

She watched his eyes a long interval. Then her auburn head tipped down and she turned back to the hotel. France caught a movement around the court-house. One of his own men came out and took station at the door, looking both ways. Ellensburg suddenly appeared in the arch of the livery stable, as solemn as a judge. France turned into Ziegler's, to find Slim Hillis waiting for him.

"I'd of come after you in another minute," muttered Slim. "The air out yonder is bad for pedestrians."

"Where's McQuarter?"

"I wish I knew. I been pluggin' all the holes around this burg to keep any of his sympathizers from pottin' you. If they try it I'll systematically take this joint apart board by board."

The doors swung and let in a man plainly agitated. He came straight to France. "Listen, Mr. France," he gulped, "I been tryin' to mind my own business, but I was told to deliver this statement to you or take a pill. Al McQuarter says for me to say that he will be at the west end of this street, waitin' for you to come out. He says for me to say it like that. He's waitin'—alone."

"Fair enough," said France, feeling sorry for the fellow. "No hard feelings, son. Go have a drink on me."

Slim Hillis had a curiously set expression on his face. He muttered something under his breath and cleared his throat. "Listen, John—

But France was shaking his head. "I know what you're going to say. It won't work. McQuarter's sending me his card and I've got to hand it back to him, personal. This is the last shake of dice, Slim. Soon done—and I'm not sorry."

He settled his belt a trifle, and looked around at the solemn faces of the men he had led through so much recent turbulence, and for a moment the pinched gravity of his cheeks relaxed to a piece of a smile. Then he stepped through the door and walked in a deliberate, unhurried stride to the center of the street. He saw the townsmen peering at him from their safe shelters, felt the warm sun beating down and the wire-

drawn silence of this still street. Turning, he faced Al
McQuarter who stood a hundred feet away, waiting.

"Good day," said McQuarter, standing in his tracks.
At this moment he seemed a slight, whipped-down
figure, impeccably dressed, as suave and imper-
turbable as a man about to get a shave. If there was
any sign of passion about him it registered only in the
slightly increased pressure of line and lip and nostril.
Nothing about the cool drawl betrayed him. He stood
there, perfect master of himself.

"You wanted to see me?" asked France.

"I believe you understand the situation, Mr. France."

"I've learned something of your intentions," replied
France evenly. "In case I'm mistaken, correct me."

"Let it stand. You have done well by yourself as a
newcomer. Congratulations."

"I am sorry to say," drawled France, "that I cannot
return the compliment."

The stillness of the street was absolute, and the soft
interchange of words ran clearly from side to side,
audible to the farthest spectator. Slim Hillis, standing
in Ziegler's doors, felt his pulse racing and a sweat
creeping into the palms of his hands. At the livery
stable, Ellensburg had bitten his cigarette into bitter
pulp. Second by second the piling up of suspense continued, cruel and torturing. Yet the principals stood
carved like relaxed statues out in the dust, calm, soft-
spoken.

"Some gentlemen," McQuarter went on in the same
liquid, casual tone, "would say you had beginner's

luck. My own opinion of you has always been high. You built up your pile of chips like an old head."

"Pleased to hear you say it, McQuarter. I regret that we can't be neighbors. I like you and if it wasn't for the fact that I stand as the challenged party I would like to brush away some misconceptions. At the risk of being unseemly I'll offer you the opportunity of laying down your gun. There's been a great deal of blood shed around here and I won't engage in another affair without going on record as trying to avert it."

"Charitably spoken," murmured McQuarter, courteously. But France saw the rising flame of the man's spirit. This could last but little longer. "However, I practically never go back on my word. Maybe we'd better get on with this business. Since I challenged you, it's your privilege to move first."

"Elect to stand and wait," France said.

"Then I bid you good day again. I'm coming forward."

He moved on, his wiry body arrow straight, boots pacing slow and measured over the interval. As he advanced yard by yard, France's eyes focused upon his swinging elbows, watching them lift perceptibly higher until the finger tips of the right hand brushed against the gun holster. The arc of swinging decreased, the man's boots began to squeak with the pressure of his springing knees. Slowly and surely France's vision narrowed, the buildings faded, the walks and porch posts dimmed into the outer haze and the world seemed to center down on that monotonously swinging gun arm.

As for himself, he had not shifted or moved a muscle. His senses had erected a barrier against every extraneous impression. He was like a piece of automatic machinery, ready to be set off by trigger pressure, disturbed by nothing outside itself, geared to one fragment of thought—to rise above the level of Al McQuarter's speed.

Then time ceased and action began, sinuous and flashing. McQuarter's gun arm came from behind the gun with an undulating move. The erect carriage broke and contorted, knees bent down, shoulders forward. The immense abyss of silence was split and shattered, the bright day's light seemed to spread and move before John France. The roar prolonged and fell off with a wake of echoes and his narrow vision widened as his eager senses embraced the full savor of life again. Walk and buildings and men and horses crowded to either side, the smell of powder smoke was in the air, a gun hung in his fist and Al McQuarter, stiffly smiling, bowed grimly at him and fell forward in the dust, hat rolling away, yellow hair bright in the sun.

Men poured out of their corners, talk welled up, nervous and high pitched. John France broke his gun, lifted the spent shell and thumbed in a fresh one, unaware that an old pattern of habit worked unconsciously for him. He looked once more at McQuarter and turned away.

Slim sprang from Ziegler's and struck him on the

shoulder, voice lifted above its normal pitch. "You broke Crowheart's crooked back. It's done—all done and I ain't sorry. Come on, get a good stiff drink."

But France shook his head and passed on to the hotel. He knew where Laurel Annison would be, so he climbed the stairs, knocked once and went in. Laurel lay face down on the bed. She sprang up at sight of him. He never knew until then what a tremendous transformation could sweep over a woman's features, nor was he ever to see so vivid a change again. She came to him, her indomitable will pressing down the dread and the horror of the last moments. Her eyes were diamond bright, searching his countenance with a queer intensity. The corners of her lips trembled slightly. All at once the color came back to her cheeks.

"I'm a little tired," France murmured. "But that's all, Laurel. The job is done."

"I thank God, John. Louise told me about Al McQuarter. She cried on my shoulder."

France shook his head. "Now let's settle that question. What's to become of you?"

"I will not answer it," she replied, turning half away.

At once the solemn and bronzed features of the man lost their weariness. He smiled. "Then I will. Come here, Laurel!"

**Center Point Publishing**
600 Brooks Road • PO Box 1
Thorndike ME 04986-0001 USA


(207) 568-3717


US & Canada:
1 800 929-9108